W9-CBG-831

THE HAUNTED TRAIL

John C Lukegord

Copyright © 2013 John C Lukegord
All rights reserved.

ISBN 13: 9781489543219
ISBN: 148954321X

Table Of Contents

CHAPTER 1

A small, ten-year-old boy roamed a few miles past his home in the backwoods of Dublin, Ireland. The path he walked was narrow with tall, green bushes along it. This boy's name was Dylan McGilicutty. Dylan had blond hair, and he wore a green hat. He was an overly curious boy who happened to wander upon a farm and a garden and noticed a giant scarecrow seemingly protecting the garden. His curiosity led him to want to steal this scarecrow on the crisp, autumn Halloween night of 1892.

Dylan, however, was unfamiliar with the scarecrow's sinister history. The scarecrow was a worship symbol to a crazy, inbred farmer named Patrick O'Sullivan. This particular scarecrow was the sacred symbol of the garden that leads to a haunted trail. It was the heart and evil soul of the garden. Other scarecrows were scattered about the garden, but none was as big and important to the crazed farmer, Patrick O'Sullivan.

Patrick had handcrafted the scarecrow. He took pride in stuffing it with hay and stitching it together with his two filthy hands. He constructed his scarecrow on Halloween, 1890. He believed the scarecrow was sacred, although it was just a silly-looking thing stuffed with hay. A few of the locals believed in what O'Sullivan preached about his sacred scarecrow. On the other hand, some of the locals thought he was out of touch with reality. The scarecrow does, however, serve as an efficient prop that keeps most of the crows away. An abundance of crows could potentially damage or ruin edible crops. The fields grow crops and are harvested so the evil that lies within this wicked area can have food.

Along Dylan's route he noticed a "no trespassing" sign, which he chose to ignore. Not far into the garden stood the sacred scarecrow, proudly hanging tall from a wooden post. In order to reach the scarecrow, Dylan had to run a few hundred yards across the field, ultimately exposing himself to O'Sullivan's watchful eye. He had to be quick and quiet because a small shed close by housed Patrick O'Sullivan.

Patrick was a former mental patient who had violent tendencies toward all living creatures. On September 7, 1870, a zookeeper caught O'Sullivan abusing a helpless sheep. People who witnessed this were very unfortunate. Patrick was warned by the zookeeper not to show his ugly face at the Dublin Zoo ever again, but Patrick didn't listen to the zookeeper's warning. He showed up at the zoo and raped this helpless sheep again. For the second time in a week the public witnessed this disgusting act. The zookeeper attempted to rescue his sheep from the clutches of O'Sullivan.

O'Sullivan had a small, metal trowel in his possession, which he had sharpened with a rock. O'Sullivan quickly drew his trowel from the back pocket of his dirty overalls and whizzed its sharpened tip across the zookeeper's throat. O'Sullivan fatally cut the zookeeper's jugular. O'Sullivan was immediately apprehended by a mob of citizens at the zoo and turned over to the authorities.

Patrick O'Sullivan was sentenced to the Dublin Mental Institution for twenty years. He was released from the Dublin Mental Institution on September 7, 1890. He was now forty-five years old. He had cultivated the evil garden for a little over two years and wore a straw hat and dirty overalls all the time. All the lights were off in the shed as Patrick rested his body from a long day in the fields. He got up at the crack of dawn daily to worship the scarecrow before his workday. He did the same thing at the end of each workday. He had a strong affinity for his worship, and not a day went by that he didn't fulfill this ritual.

He spent most of his days angrily shooting his rifle at crows attempting to fly near his sacred scarecrow. This day was no different, but his day of shooting would have an unforeseen effect on his ability to contain little Dylan. As Dylan approached the scarecrow, Patrick was just beginning to rest his eyes. Out of the corner of his eye and through a dust-stained window, he noticed Dylan crawling up the wooden post that held his sacred idol. Due to Patrick's shooting of numerous crows that day, his rifle was out of bullets. Fearing he would take too long to load his gun, Patrick furiously grabbed his pitchfork and headed out the door toward the field. His protective nature over the garden and scarecrow enabled him to move more quickly than Dylan anticipated. Dylan managed to knock the scarecrow off its post but was unable to lift the heavy idol. He noticed O'Sullivan running toward him with a pitchfork and decided to run away from the fields and toward the McArthur property.

**

Unknown to Dylan were the tendencies of the McArthur family. Scott McArthur, the head of the household, was a stern husband and father who saw himself as the sworn protector of the Dublin woods. Scott met his wife, Wendy, at a downtown Irish bar on March 17, 1878. Flanagan's Irish pub was crowded on that St. Patrick's Day. Corn beef and boiled potatoes were served as complimentary platters for the Irish pub crowd. About one hundred Dublin locals were eating and drinking in the small pub, and it was only twelve o'clock. Alcoholics were stumbling about in the pub and having a grand old time. A few altercations had occurred in the pub earlier that day. However, the disgruntled drunks responsible for the violence were escorted out. They were banned from the pub for the remainder of the St. Patrick's Day festivities.

Scott and Wendy had been dancing all day to the Irish music. A few Irishmen were playing the bagpipes to liven up the spirit in the Irish bar. When Scott first laid eyes on Wendy at the bar, he walked up to her and offered her a dance and a drink. She gave in to his politeness and couldn't resist his charm. He was a perfect gentleman to her the whole day. They were dancing in the bar, lost in each other's eyes, until the final song of the evening. Scott and Wendy got married on St. Patrick's Day, 1879, exactly one year after they first met. They got married in a small chapel and celebrated at Flanagan's afterward. Scott and Wendy moved into a small cottage a mile away from Flanagan's after they got married. A month after their marriage, Scott and Wendy quit drinking and decided to leave their good old days at Flanagan's pub behind them. They had been discussing thoughts of having two children together.

Scott fished and farmed for his daily earnings, along with building houses. He was a man of many trades who kept himself occupied. He worked very hard almost daily to support himself and his wife. His experience and hard work eventually increased his earnings. He was smart with his money. He used his

coins to pay for food and shelter. He saved every coin he could for the oppor-
tunity for a better life. He and Wendy had dreams of living in a secluded area
and raising two children. They knew their small cottage wasn't large enough to
raise a family in, and the time had come for the McArthurs to leave their small
cottage behind and pursue their dreams.

The McArthurs' dreams eventually came true, and so did their nightmares.
Mary McArthur was eight years old and petrified of her strict father. Rarely
did she aggravate her short-tempered father. She knew disapproved behavior
would result in punishment. The McArthurs' son was a ten-year-old, disobedient little brat named Billy. Billy's disobedience resulted in beatings from his
father. Scott was no longer the mentally stable person he once was. Scott had
violent tendencies toward his family and utterly dominated their lives.

A violent altercation with a cursed mummy turned him permanently insane
overnight. He was frightened years back by what he referred to as a mummy
attack. He accidentally stepped on a mummy's grave, and it rose from beyond its
grave and attacked him. On Halloween night, 1879, Scott McArthur searched
the Dublin woods to claim new property. He heard a rumor from a crazy drunk
at Flanagan's that the Dublin woods was a death trap on Halloween night. He
was unsure if the drunk at Flanagan's was telling the truth or just speaking
nonsense. Scott learned that a curse existed in the Dublin woods. McArthur
stepped on a cursed gravestone, and a mummy suddenly arose from beyond the
dead and attacked him. He claimed that the mummy wore thick, white strips of
cloth all along his body. He also claimed that the mummy's face had distorted
flesh with a hideous, bloodshot purple eye on the top of its skull. The mummy
managed to grab Scott's face and caused a devastating injury.

Eventually, Scott fled the Dublin woods and miraculously escaped from the
cursed mummy. Scott was left with a disfigured face, along with serious mental
scarring. Wendy thought that the mummy was a brief hallucination in Scott's mind.
Scott had the scars on his face, however, to prove that an altercation had happened.
Wendy's marriage then became a hostile environment. From then on, she took
verbal and physical abuse from her husband. She was coerced by her husband into
truly believing she was a pitiful human being. He turned hostile toward his wife as a
result of the overwhelming mental stress caused by the mummy attack.

The mummy attack gave him an incurable mental illness. Scott voluntarily
admitted himself into the Dublin Mental Institution because he realized his anger

and his fears frightened his wife. While McArthur voluntarily served his time in the institution, he befriended the Killington brothers. His two new friends, "The Infamous Killington Brothers," were identical twins who had served a thirty-year sentence in the Dublin Mental Institution for multiple homicides. On Halloween, 1880, they were allowed back into society. Since Scott McArthur was a voluntary patient at the facility, he could request permission to leave whenever he wanted. He planned his own release date from the institution on the same day the Killington brothers were let out. The Killington brothers were well connected with Irish evil in Dublin. Within a week of their release, the Killington brothers reconnected with lunatics they associated with years ago. McArthur showed these lunatics his deformed face and informed them that a cursed mummy was the cause of it. McArthur convinced these men that the Dublin woods were cursed.

The curses of the asylum never left this small group of men. When these men were released back into society, they assisted McArthur with his sinister plans. McArthur did not regain his grasp on reality as a result of his time in the mental hospital. He and his newfound evil crew began constructing his house and his command post on November 8, 1880. Twenty men participated in the operation and finished the construction on McArthur's land on December 31, 1880.

The command post was built on McArthur's property line for strict security purposes. The men built the fortress out of stone pillars, and it was circular in shape, fifty feet high with stone staircases spiraling from top to bottom. A turret rose from the center of McArthur's personal fortress. McArthur stood guard on his command post and monitored his property line for any potential intruders. He stood guard at his post for the majority of his time. He rigged a light atop his fortress so he could spot suspicious activity near his property line at nighttime. When the skies were dark, McArthur had a difficult time seeing through the lens of his turret. The command post was located one hundred feet away from the McArthurs' house.

Scott and his family moved into their new home on New Year's Day, 1881. Their wooden house had four small rooms. They had a small kitchen in their house as well. Ten feet outside of their house was a shack with a large bucket inside. The family used the large bucket inside of their shack to collect their urine and feces. The McArthurs had a small bucket they used to store their water supply. Wendy walked to the riverbed and filled up the little bucket with water a few times a day. The Dublin River was their source of water for cooking, sanitation, and hydration and was located about a mile south of the McArthur property line.

Soon after the McArthurs moved into their property, Scott's followers constructed small shacks in the Dublin woods and resided behind his land. McArthur's men monitored the terrain behind his property line for trespassers. They set up "kill stations" near their shacks and spread themselves throughout a three-mile perimeter in the cursed woods. These men followed the commands of McArthur and executed anyone who dared trespass on Halloween night. They referred to Scott McArthur as the "Dublin Woods Protector." Scott McArthur felt he had a strict duty to protect his property line and made sure that nobody entered or exited the Dublin woods.

**

While Dylan was escaping from his encounter with O'Sullivan by running toward the McArthur property, the McArthurs were having a dispute of their own. Little Billy McArthur, Scott's son, was constantly told not to play in the yard while his father was at his "command post." Scott felt it was extremely important to protect the integrity of the forest, and for that reason, his son was not allowed to have any fun or to live like a kid. He constantly told Billy, "Stay out of the fucking yard while I'm working."

Today was no different. Scott had a lot of trouble controlling his anger since the dreadful night the mummy attacked him. He'd been living with this mental sickness for thirteen years. Only this time Billy managed to escape from the confines of the McArthur property. Earlier this evening, Scott and Wendy had had a fight. Scott gave her a savage beating after she accidentally overcooked the family chicken dinner. At this moment, Wendy was icing down her swollen eye in the kitchen.

The children of this dysfunctional family were having a dispute of their own. They were arguing in their bedroom. Billy's younger sister Mary was pleading, "If the haunted trail doesn't kill you, Billy, Dad will!"

Billy's response was, "Fuck this. I'm getting out of this stupid family, and you should come with me! You saw the beating Dad gave Mom for ruining the chicken dinner. It's not safe here. I'm leaving and never coming back." Although Mary refused to go, Billy decided to leave anyway.

Scott heard the crash of the window breaking and decided to leave his post to chase after his nuisance of a son. "Damn it, that fucking kid," Scott said as he grabbed his spiked bat and headed down the stone spiral staircase of his fortress. After he reached the bottom of the staircase, he stormed out of his yard and after his son.

At this exact time, Dylan ran furiously onto the McArthurs' property. While on a normal day Dylan would have been shot on sight, today was a little different. Scott was no longer at his post because of his undisciplined son. Upon entering the property, the crazed farmer O'Sullivan cautioned loudly, "Dublin Woods Protector, intruder alert! I need backup!" This call fell on deaf ears as McArthur was off his post in pursuit of his son. The chase continued for Dylan into unknown Dublin territory. Dylan had never ventured this far from his house and this far into the woods. He was unaware of the fact that throughout history many people had been murdered in these cursed woods. The level of fear racing through his body led him to run faster and jump higher than he thought possible. As night fell upon them, Dylan maneuvered his way through the McArthur property and into the deep forest. The haunted trail ran directly behind McArthur's land, which left Dylan with no choice but to enter this forbidden zone.

**

Just up the path lay the shack of Matthew Killington. Killington was responsible for the Halloween Massacre of 1842. With the help of his twin brother, Martin, they managed to behead six innocent children that night. The Killington brothers decapitated the children in a field near the Dublin woods. Shortly after the murders took place, the authorities became aware of the situation and formed a manhunt in an attempt to capture the people responsible for the crime.

The Killington brothers attempted to bury all six children in the Dublin woods to cover up the murders. They managed to bury three children in the woods near the field. Halfway through their operation, the Killington brothers had to flee when the authorities spotted them in the field. When they attempted to bury the bodies, they compromised their own escape route. They were eventually caught by the Irish authorities that night and confined to a jail cell in downtown Dublin. They were transferred to the Dublin Mental Institution eight years later on Halloween in 1850.

This Halloween night happened to be the fifty-year anniversary of the massacre, and the Killington brothers had blood on their minds. Matthew was in luck this evening as he and little Dylan were on a crash course for one another. As Dylan approached, Killington heard somebody coming and hid behind a bush to see what transpired. Although it was dark, Killington managed to tackle this ten-year-old boy as he ran by the bush. Dylan had no chance, even though Killington was sixty-five years old and of small stature.

As the inbred O'Sullivan caught up to Dylan, he realized he had been captured and let out a sigh of relief. He and Killington were both bloodthirsty, and they had their prey. He shouted at Dylan, "You tampered with my scarecrow, and now you'll pay the price!" His first thought was to stick him with the pitchfork, but this idea was quickly changed when Killington pointed out his homemade guillotine. This contraption excited O'Sullivan very much. He grinned from ear to ear as he said, "Let's chop this little bastard's head off!"

Dylan now realized that his curiosity had caught up with him for the last time, and he was in real trouble now. He pleaded with the men, "Please don't kill me! I'm only a kid! I haven't done anything wrong. I'm sorry about your scarecrow, and I promise I'll make it up to you if you let me live. I didn't even take the scarecrow, so why do you want to kill me?"

O'Sullivan hastily answered, "The scarecrow is forbidden, and now you'll pay for what you've done! It fell off its post! It no longer hangs proudly! I spent countless hours handcrafting my sacred scarecrow, and you've damaged it!" O'Sullivan said to Killington, "We're wasting time! Let's drag him over to the guillotine, Killington!"

He and Killington dragged Dylan to the guillotine and prepared it for use. Tears began forming in the young boy's eyes as he realized his fate. He began to think about the ten short years that he had roamed this godforsaken corner of Ireland. As the crazed farmer O'Sullivan forced the four edges of the pitchfork into Dylan's back, it was clear that Dylan was terrified.

Now he was even more terrified as he laid eyes on the guillotine. As the men placed Dylan's neck on the guillotine, face down, one last bead of sweat ran down the young boy's face while he prepared for the inevitable. They strapped Dylan down by his hands as Killington readied his death machine. O'Sullivan's eyes lit up as he continued to poke Dylan in the back aggressively. As Dylan took a final breath, the guillotine blade was lowered abruptly, and it sliced through his little neck. His head now lay in a wooden bucket next to the guillotine.

O'Sullivan and Killington shook hands as if congratulating each other on a successful hunt. This kill completed Killington's fiftieth-anniversary night successfully. As they parted ways, O'Sullivan remarked, "Nice doing business with you. I must return to the farm and fix my broken scarecrow!"

Killington replied, "OK. I have to bury this little bastard anyways, so I will see you soon!"

As Dylan was beheaded, McArthur and his son, Billy, were having a dispute of their own. When Scott eventually caught up to Billy, he was very unhappy. He said to his son, "Look at me, you disobedient son of a bitch. The woods are cursed, and now you are. Now I must kill you before the curse of the mummy does." He swung his spiked bat and struck Billy in the head. Although Billy was already dead, McArthur continued to strike his son with the bat. Billy was now bloodied from head to torso, and McArthur finally stopped to realize what he had done. Scott walked about a mile to his property as wolves began to devour the carcass of his slain son.

CHAPTER 2

While these murderous scenes were unfolding, a group of three brothers was floating down the southern point of the Dublin River on a fishing trip. The Patrican brothers were a very close-knit family and always had one another's backs. Today would be no different. Normally these men liked to fish on the public side of the Dublin River. Their mother always told them not to go past a certain landmark on the river because of the evil that lurks beyond, but they never truly understood the significance of this advice until today. As the drunken brothers approached a "no trespassing" sign, they all looked at each other and said, "Fuck it. Let's do this."

As they pushed on further than they ever had, they heard a kind voice saying, "Turn back now. Danger is ahead. Just a friendly warning." They decided to shrug off the warning and continue. Henry Patrican was a thirty-year-old man and the oldest of the three brothers. He was a role model for his younger siblings. He had to step up and be the man of the house when his father tragically died in a horrific coal-mining accident.

His father died on April 12, 1877, which made things very difficult for the Patrican family. This shocking death devastated his mother, Sandra Patrican. She did her best to raise her three sons after her husband passed away. She passed away from natural causes on August 9, 1889.

Henry's younger brother, Wayne, was ten years old when his father died. He had a difficult time dealing with the loss of his father. He had gone fishing with his father at the Dublin River on the night before the coal-mining accident. The memory of fishing with his father at the river kept flowing through his mind during his father's funeral.

The youngest sibling of the family was a two-year-old child at the time of the father's death named Mick Patrican. Mick was a young child back then, so he only vaguely remembered who his father was. Henry was the "father figure" to his younger brothers, especially to his youngest brother, Mick. Mick Patrican had grown up since the days when he was a young, Irish lad.

The Patrican brothers were forever grateful for everything their parents did for them. The Patricans were a poor Irish family who barely made ends meet. The Patrican brothers grew up together and formed a strong brotherhood bond that could never be broken. The Patrican brothers looked alike. They had dirty blonde hair and crew cuts. They had similar builds. Wayne was the middle child, now twenty-five years old. His hobbies were drinking and fishing, and he shared these particular hobbies with both of his brothers. Mick Patrican was a small, rugged Irishman at the age of seventeen. Even Mick was unaware of the strength of this brotherhood bond.

The Patrican brothers built their boat a few years ago from scrap wood, and they took it on many fishing trips. They kept their boat in fairly good condition. The Patrican brothers caught fish from the river and sold their catch to local merchants. Fishing was their greatest passion in life and their means of survival. The Patrican brothers now took their fishing boat into the heart of forbidden territory.

A slight distance up the river stood Harry McFloyd. McFloyd was a pyromaniac growing up and had served time in the Dublin Mental Institution's Juvenile Facility for setting the grade school ablaze on Halloween, 1884. Harry was a dropout punk at the age of twelve when he committed this horrible act. He hated school and all the teachers, so he rebelled against it. With one accurate toss from a flaming bottle, Harry took out the Dublin grade school. Harry listened to the voices in his head that told him to destroy the school, but he was caught by the authorities as he tried to escape into the woods near the blazing schoolyard. He told the authorities about these evil voices in his head. The authorities sentenced McFloyd to the juvenile facility until he turned eighteen.

Just looking at this kid's smile is a nightmare. He had horrible-looking teeth and an evil smile. Harry had hideous acne all over his face and a blond mullet. He was released from the juvenile facility on April 1, 1890. He resided in a small shack near the Dublin riverbed. McFloyd was now twenty years old. He kept trespassers away from this territory of the Dublin woods. He constructed a small cannonball chamber alongside the riverbed. The cannonball chamber was built as a defense mechanism aimed toward trespassing vessels. Green bushes surround the outer perimeter of the cannonball chamber. These bushes camouflaged the cannon from approaching vessels.

Harry had a loyal four-man crew of homeless, mentally ill people who worked under his command. These men were homeless because they were too stupid to construct a shack. They lacked the knowledge and the materials to pull off such a task. Despite their inability to build a dwelling, they happened to be very good at capturing trespassers. Their hunting abilities were excellent, and that's why they were so valuable to McFloyd. They monitored the riverbed for trespassers.

As the Patrican brothers continued to sail down the river, Harry heard them and spotted the boat from a small distance away. Harry signaled to his evil crew roaming the territory nearby that trespassers were approaching. This meant that the four other guards under McFloyd's command were fully aware of a boat that was headed toward their section of the river. As the Patrican brothers drifted further down the river, Harry prepared to blast his cannonball. Harry McFloyd was a sneaky little punk, and he took ultimate pride in blind-sided cannonball attacks.

Harry quietly waited for the Patrican brothers to drift into his target range. As the boat sailed into the center of Harry's shooting range, the loud sound of a blasting cannonball echoed throughout a section of Dublin. The boat took a serious blow from the blasting cannonball. Heavily damaged, the boat listed onto its right side and was about to sink. The Patrican brothers submerged into the Dublin River along with their fishing boat. Henry yelled to his younger brothers, "We're under attack! Abandon ship!" Seconds later, his mouth filled with water as he and his brothers sank into the river.

McFloyd's security force jumped into the river. Henry and Wayne were immediately captured. Henry could not swim away quickly enough to escape. The sinking boat caused a powerful flow of current that Henry and Wayne were both caught up in. As for Mick, he remained underwater and temporarily unspotted. The four guards wasted no time dragging Wayne and Henry out of the river.

Harry ran into his small shack and grabbed a few small sets of rope. The four mental guards beat up the two oldest Patrican brothers. Henry and Wayne were outnumbered by manpower and unable to escape or defend themselves. Meanwhile, Mick was in the process of escaping from sight. Mick held his breath for nearly two minutes until he slowly raised his head above water. He slowly and silently took a couple of breaths for some desperately needed fresh air. He feared that his older brothers had both been captured.

More guards swarmed the terrain, and there was nothing he could do to save his older brothers. Henry and Wayne were being badly beaten by the swarming lunatics. In a matter of minutes, the Patrican brothers were outnumbered ten to three. McFloyd shouted, "They're guilty of trespassing on our forbidden turf, and they both must be executed! Tie these two up with my ropes immediately! As for the third trespasser on the ship, capture him and tie him up as well!"

McFloyd's crewmembers grabbed some loose rope and began to tie up Henry and Wayne. A few of the guards roamed the terrain nearby in search of the third brother, Mick. Mick quietly submerged himself again to avoid being spotted. He slowly came up for air and quietly swam toward land. He crawled out of the riverbed. The guards searched different areas nearby in attempts to capture him. Mick was a few hundred feet away from his brothers. He could see them both being tortured and dragged against their will. Mick wished he could heroically rescue his older brothers. But he couldn't help them because he was in a desperate attempt to save himself.

Henry was now being dragged against his will in the direction of the electric chair. Miles O'Neill, the designer and operator of the electric chair, waited for him. Miles was found guilty of the murder of a coworker back on April 12, 1877. Miles had a job as a supervisor in the coal-mining fields. He had a grudge against a lazy new employee who had made a critical mistake. Miles murdered the man, named Gerald Gilligan, while he was on the job.

Gerald was responsible for securing the entry to a new mine that had just been dug out and was not yet fully secured. As the diggers were attempting to exit the mine, the entryway collapsed on them, leaving them stuck in a hole thirty feet down. Miles saw this collapse, and, enraged, he pushed Gerald off the edge and into the hole. In all, twelve people died, but the remaining miners told the authorities the story about Gilligan's death. Brian Patrican was one of the fallen coal-mine workers in the horrific accident.

14

Miles served fifteen years in the Dublin Mental Institution and was released just over six months ago. Miles was fifty-two years old. He had red hair and a scruffy, red beard and lived in a small shack right next to his electric chair. The chair worked perfectly now after a few initial design flaws. Miles couldn't wait to use his death chair on the trespasser he saw captured from a distance.

Miles shouted to the guards, "Hurry up you bumbling idiots and put him in the fuckin' chair!" as Henry was being dragged closer and closer to Miles. Henry was injured and unable to escape or defend himself against the guards. Miles said, "Strap him into the chair!" The guards shoved Henry onto the electric chair. The guards punched him in the face a few times after they strapped him in. Miles secured a metal headgear set onto Henry's skull.

Miles pointed at his victim and shouted, "This is the end of your time!" He engaged the power function to his electric chair. After about a minute, the chair started to heat up. One could only imagine the horror. Henry Patrican's eyes were filled with overwhelming fear as he knew he was about to die. As his flesh started to burn, smoke rose into the dark air. Miles and the mentally disturbed guards watched from nearby. They could smell the burning flesh in the autumn air. This was the end for the eldest brother, Henry Patrican.

Mick was still a few hundred feet away and knew the fate of his brothers was not good. Wayne Patrican was being dragged against his will toward the section of the woods belonging to Douglas O'Connor.

Douglas O'Connor was a former mental patient at the Dublin Mental Institution's Juvenile Facility. Douglas and his best friend Ronald O'Leary were found guilty of beating and lynching a woman. They were convinced this woman was a sadistic witch. Based on their perception, this act seemed like no big deal to them. This hate crime occurred on Halloween, 1885 in a public section of the Dublin woods for all to see. This particular area in the Dublin woods was not considered to be cursed. Douglas and Ronald, however, roamed this area and claimed it to be their turf. The woman's name was Rosemary Mcloud. While she was practicing witchcraft in the woods around a fire, the boys ambushed her. She never saw them coming and had no chance to defend herself. She was hanged on a rope swing used by local kids for recreation.

Immediately after this attack Douglas and Ronald went to the authorities to explain what they had just done. They explained that they had killed a dangerous witch in the woods and that they did society a huge favor. Upon hearing this, the local authorities arrested and detained the two boys on murder charges. The boys were convinced that what they did was justified and saw no reason for their arrest.

Both of these punks were only thirteen years old when they committed this brutal crime. They both pleaded insanity and were sentenced to serve time in the juvenile facility. Douglas and Ronald were confined from society until they turned eighteen. The juvenile facility was a jail cell for mentally defective minors. It was fully constructed in the summer of 1880. This building was built right next to the Dublin Mental Institution. The juvenile facility became fully functional as an institution on August 22, 1880. The warden of the Dublin Mental Institution was left a vast fortune in his family will. The warden had the resources to construct the juvenile facility. The warden hired a crew, and it was built. The building was constructed with one hundred cells to contain juvenile delinquents away from society. This institution was completely full with one hundred troubled Irish youths from the ages of ten to seventeen. No mental patient over the age of seventeen was allowed to serve time in the juvenile facility. Once a mental patient turned eighteen he was either transferred to the Dublin Mental Institution or released back into society.

Ronald was brutally killed in the juvenile facility on the first day he arrived there. He was beaten to death by an angry gang because he had a tendency to run his big mouth. Ronald claimed that he was the toughest kid in the institution, but he was proven wrong when the angry lunatics ganged up on him in the showers and beat him to death.

Douglas told O'Leary that he would stick up for him if anything dangerous was to ever go down, but Douglas nervously stood back and watched as the gang beat his best friend to death. Somehow he managed to survive in the dangerous facility. After serving just less than five years Douglas was released. O'Connor and McFloyd became very close friends while they served time together in the dangerous institution. Coincidentally, they both had their parole hearing on the same day. These two mental defectives turned eighteen on the same day, April 1, 1890. On that day, they were allowed back into society. When they got out, they became part of McArthur's cult. The cult members felt that these two troublemakers were perfect young, evil blood to keep the future of the clan going strong.

For the last two years Douglas had been residing in a small shack in the Dublin woods. He had a tree with a hanging noose near his shack. O'Connor was a tall man, standing at six feet eight inches. He could reach the end of his noose with no problem standing on the ground. Douglas's kill station was located a few hundred feet away from the shack housing Miles O'Neill.

**

Douglas looked over to see the frantic kicking and screaming of a new victim. This new victim was indeed Wayne Patrican being dragged over in the direction of Douglas and the noose. Douglas said, "Dublin guards, bring this forbidden trespasser over to me immediately! I want him to suffer on Halloween just like that bitch Rosemary Mcloud!" The guards forced Wayne over to the noose, and Douglas ordered Wayne to stand on the stool beneath the rope, but he couldn't even stand up. The guards held him up on his feet because he was unable to keep his balance, as they aggressively forced this man onto the stool. Douglas walked over to Wayne and placed the noose around his neck. Wayne had a helpless look on his face. He had been badly beaten and was unable to escape or fight back. His eyes were so swollen he could barely see. His lip was so swollen he was unable to beg for his life and say his last words. Douglas pointed at Wayne and shouted, "You will be lynched for your forbidden trespass!" After that Douglas kicked the stool from under Wayne Patrican's legs. Wayne Patrican was hanged as his body and feet dangled in the air. The mental guards cheered because of another successful Halloween execution.

The guards roamed further into the terrain to search for Mick Patrican. Mick remained silent as one of the guards headed near his direction. Mick grabbed a few slabs of mud and began to cover his face and any exposed skin, making it much harder for the guards to spot him. Mick got on his hands and knees and quietly maneuvered his way around a tree to avoid being spotted. He hid behind the tree until the guard spotted nobody and eventually searched a different section of the Dublin trails.

Patrican wanted to leave this cursed section of Dublin because he knew his life was in danger, but he was way too stubborn to leave just yet. Patrican felt he must avenge the deaths of his two older brothers. He decided to move to a more secluded area. When the guards flushed out to different regions of the trail to widen their search, he would strike. He planned the murders of the electric chair operator and the man with the noose. Mick ran further into the woods. This particular section that Patrican trespassed along is where the curse of the Dublin woods originated.

As Mick moved along, he trespassed over a small patch of grass with a broken tombstone in the middle of it. Mick accidently stepped on the ancient burial ground of the cursed mummy. The mummy angrily rose from the dead and attacked him. Mick nervously jumped back when the mummy grabbed his arm. He managed to shrug off the grab and strike the mummy in his one-eyed, distorted face. The mummy dropped dead after Patrican managed to fight it off. The only harm on Patrican's body was a small red handprint on his left arm.

Mick Patrican was the only person ever to fight back against the mummy. The legend of the mummy goes back two thousand years. For two thousand years, many Irishman believed that no man could defend himself against the mummy and the terrible curses it possessed. Patrican was too determined and strong-minded to suffer from this horrific curse. It was a phenomenon that the curse of the mummy didn't affect him. As the mummy lay there dead near his two thousand-year-old grave, it faded away into thin air. When Patrican saw this, he fled the area of the cursed burial ground.

The mental guards roamed, searching the Dublin trails with lanterns in pursuit of the last surviving Patrican brother. The mentally ill who roamed suspected Patrican to be near the mummy's grave. The guards knew not to disturb the area near the mummy's grave because of the fearful curse. One of the guards had a vicious dog that Patrican could hear growling from a distance.

As the search for the last surviving Patrican brother continued, a short amount of time passed. The twelve guards searching this particular section of the Dublin trails were completely confused. Mick covered a great amount of space away from the angry mob and took cover in a small ditch. The twelve Dublin guards diverted their manpower to a different region of the trail. As Patrican emerged from the ditch, he laid clear eyes on an unguarded path that led back in the direction where both of his older brothers had recently been executed. Patrican's path for revenge was only a few hundred feet further.

Patrican tiptoed and quietly moved closer and closer to the execution station of the electric chair. He planned heavy revenge on Miles O'Neill, the electric chair operator. As Miles stood next to his post, he heard a noise from behind his shed. Miles grabbed his lantern and checked the area behind his shed. As Miles slowly rounded the corner, he held out his lantern for better night vision. Patrican ripped the lantern from out of his hands and smashed it over his face. The devastating strike to his face stunned Miles and knocked him to the ground. As Miles lay there dazed, Patrican picked him up and said, "You took away my brother. It's time for you to pay for your sins."

He threw Miles onto the electric chair and strapped him in. He strapped metal headgear over Miles's skull. Soon after, he pressed the lever of the chair to the "on" position. It took about ten seconds for the system to fully heat up, and then it did. The electric chair was still very hot from its previous use. Miles started to feel a horrible sensation of burning flesh from his self-designed electric chair. After a minute of torture, Miles was fried to his death. Douglas heard Miles's shrieks, so he ran over to see what was going on.

Patrican hid behind Miles's shack. As O'Connor moved slightly closer, he noticed that his companion had recently been fried to death. Douglas turned around and prepared to find backup. Douglas took no more than two steps when Mick emerged from out of the darkness. Mick had his small fishing knife drawn, and he managed to slit Douglas's throat. Douglas O'Connor dropped to his bloody death after the severe wound to his throat. After avenging the deaths of his two older brothers, Patrican fled the area and vanished, and he vanished quickly. He was unaware that the man he killed in the electric chair was formerly his father's foreman. When the guards spotted the smoke from a few hundred yards away, they headed toward the electric chair. When the guards all gathered, they discovered that two of their own had just been executed. Now the massive manhunt for Mick Patrican got much more intense.

CHAPTER 3

Meanwhile the annual Dublin Halloween Fair was going on about two miles outside of the no-trespassing section. A shady-looking clown of a man waited at his rigged carnival game. This man was a crooked carny as well as a burglar and a rapist. The clown wore a green suit and wig and went by the name of Herman McRandle. Herman painted his face with a white paste and dressed as a clown all the time. Herman McRandle was forty years old and was born on October 24, 1852. He didn't ever want people to see what he truly looked like. Herman liked to travel with the fair and not stay in one town for too long. McRandle had been in and out of prisons since he was a hot-tempered, young child. He stabbed a kid to death with a metal fork in his school cafeteria on Halloween. Herman dressed up as a green clown for his grade school Halloween costume party and murdered his schoolyard enemy. The name of this victim was Thurman McDaniels. This incident happened in a small town about thirty miles outside of Dublin. Herman had serious emotional issues that riled up his blood.

Herman's father had passed away on Herman's tenth birthday. He and his father were very close, and they both shared the name Herman McRandle. They both studied voodoo curses and read books on life after death. He idolized his father and felt more lost than ever after his father's death.

Herman and Thurman were mortal enemies in the schoolyard. The kids treated these two children as outcasts and forced them to fight against each other. The reason the children did this was because their names sounded so similar. They thought that it was a fun thing to do during recess. Thurman would usually get the better of Herman in the schoolyard battles. Herman would come home from school with black eyes and bruises all over his body. He outlasted his schoolyard enemy a few times.However, Thurman would usually get the better of him in combat.

Herman spent his first night in the children's orphanage on October 30, 1862. Herman had a strange dream that night. Herman's dead father revealed a deep family secret to him on the night before Halloween in 1862. His dead father spoke to him in a dream and said, "Hey, Herman, it's me, Dad. I'm sorry that I died on your tenth birthday. I told you that life exists after death. Son, you have to kill Thurman McDaniels tomorrow. The kids at school will respect you more if you kill him on Halloween. Show everyone who the McRandles are. Thurman McDaniel's name belongs on a gravestone. I believe in you, Herman. Make your old man proud. Kill that little bastard on Halloween!"

Herman woke up sweating in his orphanage bed from the night terrors. The voodoo curse corrupted Herman's mind throughout his bad dream. Herman gave in to the voice of his father from his haunting orphanage nightmare. This was the very start of his downfall as a human being.

Herman's mother was a prostitute who was embarrassed when she became impregnated by a clown. She took no responsibility for raising Herman. Herman knew his father only during his childhood. He became a carnival hustler and followed in his father's clown footsteps. Herman found ways to earn money, even when public events weren't occurring. Herman was a true hustler. He set up his booth all over the streets of Ireland and cheated the innocent.

Herman's father passed away from liver failure as a result of alcoholism on Herman's tenth birthday. Alcoholism was a serious problem in the McRandle family. As a matter of fact, Herman was intoxicated as he sat at his booth. As Herman waited to rip off a customer, he rudely shouted, "Hey, nice bust, you Irish whore!" as a woman with giant breasts strutted by. The woman with the giant breasts gave him a look of utter disgust and walked away.

McRandle said, "Come on, folks! Don't be shy! Step right up, and give it a try! It's your lucky night at the Dublin Halloween Fair!" Moments after that, an Irishman walked over to Herman's crooked booth with curiosity. This curious Irishman went by the name of Jonny Kerrigan. Kerrigan was a short and stubborn man who loved to gamble. Jonny decided to use all that was left of his spare change to give Herman's game a try.

Herman ran a crooked card game at the fair. He had fast hands when he shuffled a deck of cards. The sneaky card-shuffling trick he used was a subtle motion. McRandle would always skim his left hand slightly slower than his right hand while in shuffling motion. This unique shuffling motion caused certain cards to remain on top of the deck. Five black suit cards remained on the top. It was a very deceptive shuffling trick that Herman learned from his late father.

Herman would then place three cards down, not revealing the color of the cards. Herman knew that all three of the cards he placed down were the color black. The con artist aspect of this game is that Herman's catch phrase was "It's not that hard to pick the red card." That weasel McRandle had been scamming honest, hardworking Irish folks for years with his shabby tricks. As McRandle collected the coins from Kerrigan, he started to shuffle the deck of cards the shady way his father taught him. Kerrigan watched the way that Herman shuffled the deck. Although the motion was subtle, Kerrigan noticed a slight delay in the left hand of McRandle. Kerrigan thought for a split second that the game might be fixed. Kerrigan was a heavy gambler who loved to play poker, so he knew a shady shuffle when he saw one. Kerrigan still decided to play the game and pick a card at random. Herman placed three cards from the top of the deck on the table without revealing their suit or color. The clown said, "Are you ready, mate? It's not that hard to pick the red card. Take your time or make it quick. Either way, just take your pick." Kerrigan picked the card that was in the middle of the three.

Kerrigan pointed to the table and said, "The card in the middle, please, sir."

When Herman flipped the card over, the color was black. Herman said, "Sorry, buddy, that wasn't your round. How about another try?"

Kerrigan had already lost most of his money gambling earlier that night, and he was in a pretty foul mood. Jonny used the last of his coins to play McRandle's crooked game. Jonny quickly flipped over the other two cards and saw that they were both black. Kerrigan pointed at McRandle and yelled, "You cheated me, you crooked clown! I demand a full refund!"

Herman said, "No refunds. Maybe next time there will be three lucky red cards on the table. Come on! Wipe that grin off your face, and give it another try!"

Kerrigan gave a disgruntled look toward McRandle and shouted, "I'm broke because you ripped me off!" Kerrigan gave McRandle a vicious right jab to his big, green clown nose. Herman was dazed for a second as he prepared to fight back. McRandle struck back with a vicious head butt, which put Kerrigan to the ground in agony as Herman laughed maliciously over his fallen enemy. As Kerrigan prepared to get up, Herman grasped for his chest in some kind of attack preparation. Located on Herman's chest was a necklace holding a green flower-like emblem. This icon contained a flammable liquid that McRandle prepared just for such an instance as this. So as Kerrigan got up, Herman grabbed one of the decorative torches that were scattered around the fair. He put the torch in front of his chest while he pressed the flower containing the flammable liquid, creating a fire gun that he aimed in the direction of Kerrigan. The flame struck him on the chest and worked its way around his body, leaving no inch of his body unaffected.

As Kerrigan burned to death, McRandle smiled as he formulated a getaway route in his head. Herman tried desperately to make a getaway, but he could not run fast with the heavy green shoes he was wearing. An angry mob of concerned citizens beat him down. The citizens punched him in the face repeatedly.

Two constables quickly got involved and controlled the crowd. Officers Burnes and Nolan blew their whistles in an attempt to get the angry mob to stand down. The mob stood down as Burnes and Nolan pulled out their police clubs. They both let loose and whacked Herman's goofy-looking, green body a few times. As the police managed to put him in handcuffs, Herman shouted, "Fuck, I'm captured!"

This bizarre incident had everyone's eyes at the fair on Herman. Children at the fair were crying because they thought that a clown was supposed to be funny and not evil. McRandle held his head down in shame as officers Burnes and Nolan walked him over to the police cage connected to a horse-drawn carriage. After Herman was placed into the cage, the officers walked back over to the curious crowd. Both officers yelled out to the crowd that the carnival was closed for the evening and to exit the fair in an orderly fashion. Some people instantly ran away, while others still watched in horror. The crowd eventually scattered from the fair as the carnies closed down their crooked operations for the evening.

**

The chariot horse transported the clown a few miles up the road to the Dublin Mental Institution. Burnes and Nolan were officers at the institution who had been assigned to public duties for the Dublin Halloween Fair. They'd been working at the institution for twelve years. They were both rugged Irishmen and very experienced constables. They were both builders before they became officers. These men constructed the Dublin Mental Institution's juvenile facility. When Burnes and Nolan met the warden of the facility, they formed an immediate friendship. The warden was very impressed with the architectural design of the juvenile facility. He thought the whole hired crew did an excellent job. The warden convinced Mr. Burnes and Mr. Nolan to join the Dublin authority force. Within a year, Burnes and Nolan gave up their jobs as construction workers. The warden personally trained them and hired them as constables at his facility. He felt as though they would be an asset to the establishment. Burnes and Nolan have served proudly for the last twelve years. Since their twelve years on the force, they have become more arrogant and occasionally corrupt.

Herman was very pissed off; however, he strangely enough sat very patiently in the back of the chariot. Herman said to the officers, "I'm going to bust out of this prison tonight and cause a ruckus in these fuckin' woods!"

Officer Nolan looked back at Herman and said, "We will shoot you if you cause any problems with us or the other mental patients."

The clown stated, "I would love to eat a bullet! When I die, I'll fuck with you in the afterlife!"

Officer Nolan lit a cigar and said, "Whatever, you stupid, wimpy clown."

The clown said, "Hey, can I score a cigar?"

Officer Nolan said, "Sorry, you're shit out of luck, clown. Now shut the hell up back there, or I'll club you again!"

McRandle sat quietly with his evil thoughts as the chariot headed slowly to the institution.

CHAPTER 4

Back at the Dublin trails, the Evil Chef Scumbag was preparing his station for the big stew. Charles O'Callahan was a former mental patient at the Dublin Mental Institution. He was a man of a heavy frame and was forty-eight years old. He had a passion for reckless cooking and a big appetite.

He was an unsanitary, stubborn chef at the Dublin Elementary School until he lost his job and his mind. O'Callahan got into an argument with his coworker Jerry O'Riley and murdered him in front of the students when O'Riley disagreed with O'Callahan's culinary methods. He did not like the way he butchered the cows because he thought that the food the children ate should be treated properly. Obviously, O'Callahan did not agree because he butchered Jerry to death on June 12, 1875. This act of manslaughter happened on the last day of the school year. It was a terrible thing for the school children to witness before starting their summer vacation. They all had a look of horror on their little faces when O'Riley bled to death on the dirty kitchen floor.

Charles O'Callahan served fifteen years in the Dublin Mental Institution for this act of human slaughter. He served as the head chef at the institution for the fifteen years he was imprisoned. He was allowed back into society on June 12, 1890. He joined the evil tribal cult of the Dublin woods. The cult proudly took this man in for his culinary value. He resided in a small shack in the Dublin woods right near his unsanitary workstation. Charles was the head chef of the haunted trail. He cooked meals for all the lunatics residing in the Dublin woods. He often received vegetable donations from the crazed farmer O'Sullivan.

The eastern section of the trails was where former mental patients roamed for animals and trespassers. This particular group of former mental patients worked under the command of O'Callahan. Once either a person or small animal was captured it was usually thrown into a barricaded cage. A few raccoons were being transferred from the cage and into O'Callahan's stew. The mentally ill have known tendencies for being cannibals. They love the taste of a raccoon or a trespasser in O'Callahan's stew. These former mental patients heavily guarded the no-trespassing zone.

A married couple walked slightly past their house in the backwoods of Dublin, Ireland. They were both dressed up as green pirates, wearing black pirate hats and black patches over their left eyes. They both enjoyed Halloween in a festive way and couldn't stand the sadistic side of it. Holly and Harold McBrier held hands as they enjoyed their walk.

Holly and Harold were very peaceful people, both raised to treat people with respect. The McBrier's were a small sized couple. They both stood just under five feet tall and had short dark brown hair. The McBriers took pride in their Irish Protestant faith.

Harold proposed marriage to Holly in this particular section of the Dublin woods the previous year on Halloween night. They wanted to have a celebration one year later in the same section of the woods, wearing the same Halloween costumes. They wanted to get out of the house and have a romantic picnic in the woods where Harold had proposed. The couple had common sense and knew not to walk much further into the Dublin woods. They stopped walking about a quarter of a mile outside of the no-trespassing section of Dublin. They walked to the exact spot where the proposal took place.

Harold put down his picnic basket and took his wife into his arms. They began to kiss as they slowly dropped to the ground and got more comfortable. One of O'Callahan's guards had wandered past the no-trespassing section in pursuit of Patrican. What this ill-minded person heard from a distance was the couple making noises. When he approached, he saw them kissing on the ground. He lost focus on Patrican and roamed back to where more of his companions were. The guard informed his companions of lurking trespassers positioned in the eastern section of the woods. The news spread fast among O'Callahan's crewmembers. Within a few minutes, five men representing O'Callahan's crew swarmed over to the public section to disturb the romance.

The McBriers thought that they would be safe as long as they didn't roam too deep into the Dublin woods, but they had made a bad judgment call and compromised their safety. O'Callahan's crewmembers swarmed them and accused them of trespassing. The McBriers nervously told the lunatics confronting them that the section they were in was for the public. When the guards had heard enough of the McBriers' remarks concerning the public boundaries in Dublin, one of O'Callahan's men shouted, "You're in our section of Dublin, and you'll pay the ultimate price for trespassing in these woods!"

The nervous McBriers got pinned down, face first in the dirt and tied up with their hands behind their backs. The helpless couple yelled and screamed for help, so the guards tied a cloth around their mouths. The McBriers were now completely unable to scream for help. Evil was among them, and no one was around to save them from it. They tried to shake their way free and escape, but both failed, and their attempts enraged the guards even more. The guards yanked them off the ground and forced them to O'Callahan's prep station of death. The treacherous walk from the picnic to O'Callahan's station took about three minutes.

The Evil Chef Scumbag waited to cook them in the stew. The Chef said, "No need to throw these two lurking trespassers in the cage! The stew is ready for them! The taste of two trespassers along with O'Sullivan's vegetables will make a hearty broth! Ladies first!" The Chef pointed his dirty knife right at Holly. The guards dragged Holly over to the Chef. The Chef forced Holly to lie down face up. She was strapped in the center of the Evil Chef's prep station. Her husband watched from nearby as O'Callahan beheaded her with a butcher knife. Her head was tossed into the stew as Harold grieved for the loss of his soul mate.

Holly's body was hacked up by the evil chef and thrown into the horrible stew. Now it was time for Harold McBrier's execution for his forbidden trespass. O'Callahan pointed his bloody knife at Harold and said, "Now it's time for you to share the same fate as your wife, you forbidden trespasser!" O'Callahan's crew of guards threw Harold onto the Chef's cutting board. He suffered the same process as his wife before him. The poor and innocent McBrier couple paid the ultimate price for roaming the public section of the Dublin woods. The Evil Chef Scumbag and his motley crew of evil guards laughed as they executed a couple completely innocent of trespassing.

CHAPTER 5

On the northern peak of the trail, three young Irish punks hiked up the back section of the mountain to cause mischief to the hermit residing atop. These three boys were all Dublin locals and were twelve years old. Their names were Robert Flannagan, Dennis Fitzpatrick, and Hank McManis. They all went to school together in Dublin and had a taste for mischief on this crisp Halloween evening. All three of these kids were dressed up in black for the high mountain mission.

Robert pressured his friends to go on a daring mission atop the mountain with him. He told his friends that a mountain dweller lived on the top of the Dublin Mountain in a small hut. His friends became overcurious after hearing this news, and they had to see the mysterious mountain dweller with their own eyes. All of these Irish children lived within a mile of the mountainside. Robert lived half a mile away from the mountainside in a small house with his family.

His family had remained safe from the curses of the Dublin woods for as long as they had resided nearby. Robert was the only child of Christopher Flanagan and Francine Flannagan. Francine and her husband owned Flanagan's Irish Pub downtown. Their pub has been in service for twenty years. They were both forty-five years old and cherished their only son. Their son worked as a busboy at Flanagan's Pub and did chores for his family after school. The local drunks at Flanagan's thought that Robert was adorable. Robert was courteous and attentive as a busboy. However, outside of his busboy duties at Flanagan's, Robert was a little Irish renegade. For the past week, Robert had been sneaking out past his bedtime and roaming the northern peak of the mountain. The lunatics who roamed the Dublin woods focused none of their manpower on the trails lining the mountainside.

The hermit was sleeping while the children wandered onto his territory. Unlike the other lunatics in the Dublin woods, the hermit was never a formal mental patient. He was an angry mountain dweller who hated trespassers. The guards never bothered the hermit, and the hermit never bothered them. It was a mutual bond of respect between the hermit and the mentally ill.

The hermit had long, grungy hair and a scruffy, brown beard. He was filthy and refused to bathe in the Dublin River down below the mountain. His stench was unbearable. Conceived atop the Dublin mountain, Othello Hanlon had lived there all of his life. He was raised to be a hermit from the day he was conceived.

Robert Flanagan brought his schoolbag containing a carton of eggs and a set of bolt cutters. Robert opened his bag and took out the items, which he showed off to his friends. His friends were amazed when they saw the bolt cutters and the carton of eggs. Robert said to his friends, "I've been staking this place out all week. Let's egg this fuckin' mountain dweller." Robert used the bolt cutters to cut a crawlspace perimeter through the metal barbed-wire fence. A sudden change of emotion then happened with Robert's friends. They both got a bad feeling about the high, dark mountain mission.

Dennis said, "Something about this place seems a little off to me. I think the mountain dweller who lives up here doesn't want us vandalizing his territory."

Hank replied, "I think you're right, Dennis. This place seems a little sketchy. Pissing off this mountain dweller could turn out ugly for us. We don't know who he is and what he's capable of. We don't belong up here. We should head back down the mountain and go home. Or we could go back to the fair and try to win our money back from that crazy clown."

Robert yelled at both of his friends and said, "Don't you two back down on this mission! We didn't climb up all this way just for nothing! I say we egg this fuckin' mountain dweller and send a message! We don't want this shithead dwelling on our mountain! I'm almost finished forming the crawlspace! Let's go, girls! We don't have all night!"

After a few minutes of multiple chops with the bolt cutters, a crawlspace was formed. Hank and Dennis gave in to Robert's peer pressure in fear of being deemed afraid. The three punks now had access to the evil hermit's property. They crawled through the perimeter and entered the hermit's lair. The three little renegades grabbed the eggs from out of the carton and began bombarding the hermit's rotting shack. A barrage of eggs hit the hermit's rotted high-rise shack.

The hermit awakened from his sleep and stepped outside of his small hut. He stared down at the three troublemakers and shouted, "Who dares disturb me in my slumber!"

Robert shouted at the hermit and said, "I hate you, you fuckin' bum! We don't want you living in Dublin! Get the hell off our mountain!" Then he picked up a rock and threw it at the hermit's head.

Robert just took the practical joke of throwing eggs to a whole new level when he threw the rock. Robert and his friends laughed for a few seconds as if they won the territorial dispute against the hermit and demoralized him. Othello, however, wasn't demoralized at all. He was more enraged than he'd ever been before. The hermit looked down at the three troublemakers and shouted, "Big mistake, you little bastards! The Dublin Mountain is my domain! You're all fuckin' dead!"

The hermit leaped off of his small porch and lunged toward Robert. Othello grabbed a rock he saw on the ground and bashed it on Robert's face. Robert experienced a devastating blow to the side of his little skull and was now completely unconscious. Hank and Dennis witnessed their friend's serious injury and were both frozen in fear. The hermit looked angrily at Hank and Dennis as he pointed his dirty finger toward both of them. He got up and hunted them down. Dennis said in panic, "Retreat back to the fuckin' crawlspace!"

Dennis and Hank turned their frozen fear into rapid movement. They both made a desperate attempt to flee the hermit's lair. The hermit eventually caught up to them. When he did, he bashed both of their skulls together. This blow by the hermit knocked both of them unconscious. Unfortunately, these two children were only a few feet away from the crawlspace that Robert had created. It took a few minutes, however, the hermit managed to gather up all three of the unconscious children. Then Othello grabbed a rope and tied all three of the unconscious children to a tree. The evil hermit gathered rocks, sticks, and leaves to form a fire pit. The hermit struck a match and started to light the fire pit.

Seconds later, a fire was lit directly under the three bound children. The three boys regained consciousness and realized they were all burning. The children panicked and cried as they realized they were being burned to death. The hermit laughed with an evil intent as he said, "Happy Halloween, you little bastards! Welcome to your new grave!" The three boys burned to death.

The hermit grabbed a filthy blanket he kept outside and used it to smother the fire. He also used this blanket to smother the burning children. He untied the three children from the tree and dragged them one by one toward his gate. The hermit raised his hands in the air and gave his Irish chant to open the evil gate: "Oh mighty gate of the Dublin Mountain, I command you to open!" As a sudden bolt of heat lightning struck into the air, the gate started to rise slowly.

The gate fully opened up as the hermit rolled the dead children one by one down a slope of the mountain. The slope was a two thousand-foot drop onto a lower section of the Dublin trail. The dead children's bodies took about fifteen seconds to fall before landing brutally on level ground. The hermit's gate slowly closed from above as wolves began to devour the flesh of the three burned children.

CHAPTER 6

On the mountainside of Dublin, roughly a few miles away from the hermit's lair, is the Dublin Mental Institution. This building is adjacent to the juvenile facility. The Dublin Mental Institution is a highly secured prison for mental defectives who are over the age of eighteen. This institution contains Irish lunatics, as does the Dublin woods. The only difference is that these mental patients are confined from society. The Dublin Mental Institution was fully constructed on August 22, 1850. The architects involved in the construction made several mistakes along the way and eventually fixed them. Several architects injured themselves during the exhausting construction. The construction of the building posed many problems throughout the building process.

There was a mandatory twenty-four hour lockdown for all convicted prisoners. This mandatory lockdown rule also stood for volunteer patients who'd committed themselves into the institution. The prisoners were denied the privilege of breathing fresh air although they could see it through metal-barred windows. The security features in the building were very advanced. The state-of-the art security features made escape from the premises very difficult. Privileged officers on duty at the institution possessed master prison keys. These keys were able to lock and unlock the main doorway and all of the cell rooms. Although individual cells stayed unlocked during lockdown, access in and out of the building was prohibited. Inmates' rooms were locked only if they were confined to solitary.

The Dublin Mental Institution had a haunting history throughout its existence. An evil, white ghost, known as the Ghost of Cornelius, floated high in the air over the cursed asylum as McRandle approached from a distance. This evil ghost floated by as a warning sign because things were about to go from bad to worse. The Ghost of Cornelius was an evil spirit among the Dublin woods that had existed for the last twenty-three years. There's a myth that a friendly spirit has the supernatural ability to keep a boundary on the Ghost of Cornelius. A few Irish folks believe that a friendly spirit traps the Ghost of Cornelius in the Dublin woods and spares the rest of Ireland.

The Ghost of Cornelius was an Irishman before he died and became a ghost. Cornelius Walsh and Michael Patrican were the two most experienced fishermen in all of Ireland. They were rival fishermen for almost a decade. In October of 1850, Cornelius and Michael sailed the seas of Northern Ireland on separate missions in hopes to find a promising swell of fish. Cornelius was disgruntled and having no luck at all catching fish. He sailed toward the coastline, hoping that his luck would change. After having no luck, he docked his boat on the sand and took a hiatus from fishing.

Michael had a successful day of fishing and eventually ran out of live bait. He was a few miles away from the shoreline when he headed toward land to gather up more bait. Michael noticed a small fishing vessel beached on the sand while he was sailing toward the coastline. He was curious about the boat for a few seconds before turning his attention to the job of getting more bait. He had no idea the fishing boat belonged to his enemy. When Michael approached the small shoreline beach, he anchored his vessel on the edge of the coastline next to a giant rock. After he secured his boat, he grabbed his minnow trap and stepped off his boat. When both of his feet hit the Irish sand, he saw his enemy eye to eye for the first time.

Michael Patrican saw his rival for only a split second before he was blindsided and killed by him. Cornelius had hidden behind the giant rock off the shoreline when he noticed Michael's vessel approaching and remained hidden behind the rock while Michael docked his boat on the shoreline. Cornelius crept quietly around the rock with a small knife in his right hand when he noticed Michael preparing to step off his boat. Cornelius gave Michael no time to react when he came from behind the rock and slit his throat. On the night of October 11, 1850, Michael Patrican was murdered. He was also decapitated and Cornelius took the head with him upon fleeing. He was the Patrican brothers' grandfather. The brothers never met their grandfather because he died before they were all conceived.

After Cornelius Walsh murdered his enemy, he set sail on his fishing boat and fled the area. Not long after he set sail, a couple, George and Mindy Kelly, was walking the beach not far from where the murder had just occurred. The Kellys met on this beach in their early childhood and became the best of friends. They met when they were five years old and grew up on the beach together. The beach was still their favorite spot to spend their leisure time.

The beach was five miles long, and in the midst of their travels, they noticed a man dead on the ground next to a fishing boat. The Kellys immediately fled the beach and alerted the authorities. Within minutes, the authorities organized a massive search in hopes of catching the murderer. Twelve constables searched the beach and the northern Irish Sea. Six constables searched the beach, and the other six constables took a vessel and searched the sea. When the constables sailed ten miles offshore, they spotted a man rowing a small boat in the middle of the ocean. The man the constables spotted was Cornelius Walsh.

Cornelius started paddling as hard as he could when he knew the constables had spotted him from a distance. The six constables were rowing their vessel much faster then Cornelius could and gained on him. When the constables rowed within one hundred feet of their target, two of them pulled out shotguns and opened fire on Cornelius. Cornelius heard shots being fired at him and abandoned ship. Cornelius submerged into the ocean and tried to swim away. Cornelius's small fishing boat was struck with a few bullets when the constables missed their target. Two of the constables jumped into the sea in an attempt to capture their fleeing suspect. The four other constables watched and waited for their suspect to emerge from the ocean.

Cornelius was underwater for about a minute until he ran out of breath and emerged from the cold swells of the choppy Irish ocean. When he emerged, the two constables in the ocean were within ten feet of him. They swam toward him quickly and managed to apprehend him. The constables searched Walsh's boat and found Michael Patrican's decapitated head. Cornelius Walsh was found guilty of the murder of Michael Patrican. He was sentenced to the Dublin Mental Institution for twenty years. He was the first man ever committed to the Dublin Mental Institution. He served nineteen of those twenty years and died of natural causes at the age of fifty-four on Halloween, 1869.

CHAPTER 7

The police chariot horse arrived at the Dublin Mental Institution. Burnes and Nolan walked to the back of the cage and opened the back latch. They noticed that the clown was passed out and drunk as a skunk. Officer Nolan pulled out his baton. He quietly whispered to his partner, Burnes, "I'm going to club this goofy bastard one more time just because it's Halloween." Officer Nolan gave a vicious club attack to Herman's ribcage. The clown felt the fierce blow, gasped for air, and slowly got up.

Burnes said to Nolan, "You always were a true class act." Burnes and Nolan both laughed with a sneer because the clown was a scumbag. The two of them slowly escorted the shackled clown inside of the Dublin Mental Institution and down the hallway, into the criminal-processing room of the facility. Thomas Roberts, the warden of the Dublin Mental Institution and the juvenile facility waited in the office. He served as a guidance counselor for the mental patients and determined the fate of prisoners with parole hearings. His father was the previous warden at the Dublin Mental Institution. He died on September 16, 1872, and left the position to his son Thomas in the family will. Thomas buried the corpse of his father behind the institution.

From then on, constables who passed away were buried behind the Dublin Mental Institution in a gated cemetery in honor of their service. The Ghost of Cornelius haunted the graveyard behind the institution every year on Halloween night. It sought revenge for the years he was confined to the asylum. Thomas was a constable at the institution when his father was in charge. He and his father spent many days and nights at a private shooting facility in the institution. Thomas and his father both had developed long-distance shooting skills through years of practice, but, ultimately, they had a knack for it. Thomas was a corrupt warden who wasn't afraid to break the regulations of the institution once in a while.

Burnes and Nolan escorted the clown into Dr. Roberts's office. As Dr. Roberts and McRandle stared each other in the face, there was a moment of awkward silence. Dr. Roberts said, "Herman McRandle. We meet at last. I'm glad you're here. Society can do without you. Welcome to the Dublin Mental Institution." McRandle stood there with a disgruntled look on his white face.

Officer Burnes said to the warden, "Sir, this man is guilty of murder. He burned an innocent man to death at the Dublin Halloween Fair. He was captured before he could escape."

The warden said, "Good job, gentlemen. I knew I could count on you."

Officer Burnes said, "The angry mob at the fair deserves half the credit as well, sir. They captured him before we did."

The warden replied, "I'm sure they do, Officer Burnes. Their bravery, along with their successful efforts in restraining this lunatic is much appreciated." The warden said to McRandle, "I've seen your profile, Mr. McRandle, and I've talked to other prison wardens all over Ireland. They warned me about your bullshit, and we won't stand for it in this institution. There's no trial or freedom for you anymore. Your days of hustling innocent folks at the Dublin Halloween Fair are long gone.

"Herman McRandle, you are hereby sentenced to the Dublin Mental Institution for life. You will report to your cell on the fifth floor in cell number four-ninety-nine. You are the only criminal residing on this top level. We have stairwells at all four corners of the building. We have a strict policy in this institution. There is a mandatory twenty-four hour lockdown for all convicted prisoners. Our facility holds five hundred rooms. However, there are approximately two hundred mental defectives currently serving time here. I don't want you causing any trouble, McRandle. That's why I'm secluding you.

"The cafeteria is open for five more minutes, and then the warning bell will ring. After the bell rings, you have five minutes to report back to your assigned cell. You act up once, and I'll personally put a bullet in your skull. Remember, Mr. McRandle, we have the guns, and you're a piece of dog shit. I dare you to make a move."

Herman angrily replied, "Fuck you and your bullshit rules, Roberts! I plead insanity! I dare you to pull the trigger! When I die, my evil spirit will live on and fuck with your sanity!"

Dr. Roberts said, "I don't believe in ridiculous superstition theories involving ghosts and evil spirits, Mr. McRandle. Officer Nolan, club this pitiful clown a few times and get him the fuck out of my sight."

Officer Nolan whacked the clown with his baton a few times as Herman screamed in pain and braced himself. Dr. Roberts said, "Thank you, Officer Nolan. You just made my night. I need another quick favor as well. I need you and Officer Burnes to check on Samuel McTavish. Please make sure that he gets his food and his medicine."

The officers simultaneously said, "Yes, sir, Dr. Roberts." Burnes and Nolan escorted the clown out of Dr. Roberts's office and down the main hallway. The two officers used their keys to take the shackles off the clown.

Officer Burnes said to Herman, "Remember what Dr. Roberts said about our strict policy. Don't you try to pull any bullshit, McRandle. We're the ones who are in control now."

Officer Nolan said, "The cafeteria is straight ahead, and you have five minutes to get something to eat. Oh, by the way, the food sucks here!"

Herman walked toward the cafeteria with a shit-eating grin on his face as he slowly turned his clown head back and said, "Hey Burnes, Nolan, I'm bullshit about those club attacks. I'll get my revenge when you both least expect it." The officers shrugged off McRandle's threat and calmly walked away.

**

Herman entered the cafeteria just before access to the mental patients was no longer allowed. As he approached the greasy mental chef, he looked at him and said, "Hey, greaseball, let me get some corn beef and some of those shitty-looking mashed potatoes. I'm starving."

The greasy chef served the clown exactly what he had suggested for a meal. McRandle accepted his disgusting plate of food from the scummy chef and walked over to an empty table and sat down. Many of the mental patients were obsessively gazing at him. His clown outfit made him the center of attention. The cafeteria was very quiet with the exception of soft whispers from raving lunatics. His recent arrival at the institution made the mental patients extremely curious.

McRandle was a good con artist, and he wasn't even hungry at all. What McRandle did was very clever and sneaky. He managed to pocket a metal fork that was provided with his meal. Herman looked around the cafeteria and noticed that other mental patients were staring at him. Herman said, "Fear no evil, men! Burnes and Nolan are going to die tonight!" The mentally ill around the room were all in shock to hear what McRandle had to say. No more than a few minutes later the bell rang and feeding time for the prisoners was over.

Out of all of the mental patients, there was one man who was now truly afraid. The petrified man who overheard McRandle's threats was Walter McFrancis, a thirty-year-old paranoid schizophrenic who feared the everyday world. He was a frail-boned man with light brown hair. He was very easily intimidated when he witnessed or experienced any kind of danger. Walter turned himself into this institution voluntarily after his mother died when he was twenty-eight. He never knew his father because the man abandoned him when he needed a father figure. Being around his mother all the time turned him into a big momma's boy. When she passed away, he could not take care of himself properly anymore. Although Walter was physically healthy, he suffered from mental illness. McFrancis also suffered from a severe case of insomnia. He decided it was best for him to now reside here. Most of the inmates at the facility often referred to Walter as a "pussy." McFrancis had never been physically abused by the harassing inmates due to the strict policy that is enforced by the warden of the facility.

Walter thought there was something very dangerous about the clown but tried to ignore the situation and block it out of his mind.

While the mental patients were leaving the cafeteria, Burnes and Nolan headed down to the basement science lab to check on Samuel McTavish. Burnes and Nolan had multiple responsibilities during tonight's shift. McTavish was a bitter mental patient who caused unnecessary chaos in the cafeteria. On October 1, 1892, Samuel McTavish started a fight with a mental patient named Chester O'Ryan in the cafeteria. Officer Jones saw McTavish throw his meal at Chester. When McTavish's scrambled eggs and corn beef hash hit O'Ryan square in the face, a massive food fight began.

O'Ryan became enraged over this and charged at McTavish. O'Ryan shoved McTavish off of the cafeteria bench and began to choke him with his hands. Within a few seconds, McTavish broke free from the chokehold and started throwing punches at O'Ryan's face. O'Ryan took a few punches, but before he was able to throw a few punches of his own, Officer Jones jumped on top of McTavish to break up the fight.

McTavish lashed out at Officer Jones instead of submitting to him. Officer Jones fell and hit his skull on the cafeteria floor. Officer Jones was injured, and the food fight in the cafeteria got more chaotic. There were two-dozen constables in the cafeteria trying to restrain patients during the food fight. Four constables clubbed McTavish within seconds of Officer Jones's head injury. O'Ryan was restrained by the constables but not beaten. Ten more constables soon arrived at the cafeteria for backup. The food fight lasted around five minutes before the constables took control. Officer Jones suffered a mild head injury and missed a few days of work.

Chester O'Ryan was proven not to be at fault for the altercation with McTavish. McTavish was proven to be the one responsible for provoking the food fight, along with the assault on Officer Jones. The mental patients had to clean up the mess they caused in the cafeteria as punishment. Dr. Roberts then put McTavish in the solitary confinement unit of the facility. McTavish was an annoyance and constantly shouted, "Let me the fuck out of this cage! I'm a human being! You can't treat me like this!" Dr. Roberts couldn't take McTavish as a problem anymore, so he went against regulations. Dr. Roberts had studied science and the traits of human anatomy. He used a tranquillizer to take McTavish down. Once McTavish passed out, Dr. Roberts did illegal scientific tests on him.

According to the facility regulations, the normal protocol for punishing a problematic patient is solitary confinement. Dr. Roberts took away Samuel's rights and went against protocol. One could call Dr. Roberts a human devil. Samuel was Dr. Roberts's experimental lab rat. Dr. Roberts had a sinister plan to create a genetically altered human for prison security purposes. Had this experiment been successful, Dr. Roberts's wish would have come to fruition. Instead, Samuel McTavish became permanently disfigured, and he grew a third eye on the left side of his face. His left arm shrank while his right arm grew twice its normal size. Samuel McTavish was permanently disfigured. He would remain a freak in a cage for the rest of his pitiful life.

Loud noises echoed from below as Burnes and Nolan walked further down the basement steps. The basement level was extremely dark. Officer Burnes shone a small candlelight lamp ahead of them as they cautiously walked down the stairwell. The officers reached the bottom steps of the basement level. As they walked toward the secured cage, McTavish shouted, "Officer Burnes, Officer Nolan! You need to release me at once! Dr. Roberts has gone way too far with these illegal experiments on me! My body is changing form, and I can't stop vomiting! I'm nauseous all the time, and it smells horrendous down here! I'm living in my own filth! I'm dizzy, and I have a massive headache! I don't feel right! I'm a human being! You can't treat me like this! I need to breathe fresh air! This cage and this medicine are causing me to go insane! I have my rights! Release me now!"

Officer Burnes said, "You lost your rights when you attacked Officer Jones! You're lucky you're still alive, McTavish!"

Samuel hissed at Burnes and Nolan from inside of his dirty cage. There was a disgusting bucket of fish scraps located in the basement. The fish scraps had been left in the basement overnight, discarded from last night's dinner. Officer Burnes grabbed the bucket of disgusting fish scraps. Officer Nolan clubbed the cage and told McTavish to stand down. Officer Nolan pulled out a tranquilizer gun and pointed it at McTavish. Officer Nolan began to open the cage while still pointing his tranquilizer gun at McTavish.

As McTavish quietly stood down, Officer Nolan opened the cage. As soon as the cage was fully opened, Officer Burnes dumped the bucket containing unsanitary fish scraps all over Samuel McTavish. At this exact time, Officer Nolan shot him with his tranquilizer gun. McTavish immediately passed out after he was shot with a tranquilizer from his opened cage. This freak show of a man would now be unconscious for about eight hours.

Officer Nolan said to Officer Burnes, "Hey, Burnes, I think that scumbag McTavish was right. It does smell horrendous down here. I'll give this freak a little Halloween shower." Officer Nolan urinated all over McTavish as he was passed out and unaware of the further abuse. As the two officers began to laugh, Officer Nolan finished urinating on McTavish. Officer Nolan shut the door to the treacherous cage. They gave Samuel McTavish his food and his medicine upon the request of Dr. Roberts and finished their corrupt business down in the basement.

They headed back up the long flight of stairs. Officer Burnes was lighting the dark hallway with his candlelight lamp so the two of them could see. Other prison guards were escorting some of the more dangerous patients back to their cells. Burnes told Nolan, "I need to track down McRandle and escort him to his cell. The bell rang five minutes ago. I hope he's not clowning around somewhere in the building against our command. If he is, I'll club him again."

Officer Nolan said, "I have to go back to the chariot horse. I forgot my cigars in there. I'll help you find McRandle when I get back."

The two of them went in their own directions. Officer Burnes began his search for McRandle on the fifth floor. Once he reached the fifth floor, he briefly checked the hallway and saw no one in sight. After his cursory hallway sweep, he took a peek in the closed door of cell number four-ninety-nine. What Officer Burnes saw through the barred window was the illusion of a brilliant con artist. By his own two eyes, it appeared that the door was closed and the clown was safely in his cell. Officer Burnes saw a bed in the left corner of the small cell with a bulging blanket and a green clown wig on top of a pillow. As he turned around, he heard a giggle just as he was stabbed in the throat with the previously pocketed fork.

Herman had remained unseen before he struck Burnes with the fork. He grabbed the key set inside of the wounded guard's pocket. Herman opened the door to his assigned cell, grabbing his green clown wig and putting it on his head. After that, he dragged the severely injured Officer Burnes into the cell and locked him in. Herman kept the keys on him to make escape impossible for the dying guard.

As Herman started to walk to the stairwell, he knew he had to be sneaky and unseen. Herman managed to walk down the long stairwell with no other officers in sight. All of the officers were doing sweeps along the hallways and monitoring the other potentially dangerous prisoners. Once McRandle reached the first floor, he sneaked around the corner near the front door of the building. The guard assigned to that section of the first floor was Officer Nolan. He had just returned to his stationed post after quickly grabbing his cigars. Officer Nolan heard something in the corner of the building and decided to take a quick look. As he looked around the corner he heard the word "Boo" as McRandle stabbed him in the throat with the stolen fork.

McRandle frisked the injured officer and stole his handgun, tucking the stolen handgun in the back of his goofy clown outfit. One of McRandle's styles of attack was close kills with a fork. By killing in this manner, he relived violent moments in his head from his dark childhood past.

Walter McFrancis was still up and had witnessed the attack through the barred window of his cell. Walter was terrified and did not make a sound. After stabbing Nolan with the fork, Herman walked to the main door. He inserted the master key into the lock and opened the door. Herman McRandle walked out of the Dublin Mental Institution. The angry clown had vowed his revenge on Burnes and Nolan, who both bled to death. McFrancis was the only witness, and the clown didn't even know it.

McFrancis peeked out his metal guarded window and saw the clown flee and vanish into the Dublin woods. Walter McFrancis started to yell, causing a loud, frantic scene inside of his cell. The officer commanding the area just around the corner of the same floor heard the noise Walter was making. Officer Jones ran over from around the corner of the building to see what the noise was about and to investigate the problem.

Once he rounded the corner, he noticed the dead body of Officer Nolan. Officer Jones nervously asked Walter, "Did you see what happened?"

Walter said, "The clown went nuts, killed Officer Nolan, and escaped into the woods. I saw him out my window. I want to talk to Dr. Roberts about this."

Officer Jones said, "OK, Walter. Try to stay calm. I'll run to his office and inform him of the situation!" McFrancis had known Dr. Roberts longer than he had known Officer Jones, so he was much more comfortable speaking with him.

Officer Jones hustled down the hallway of the facility to Dr.Roberts's office and knocked on the door. Dr. Roberts unlocked the door and said, "What's the matter, Officer Jones?"

Officer Jones replied, "Sir, Officer Nolan is dead, and Officer Burnes is missing. They were on their way to check on McRandle just five minutes ago. I think that McFrancis kid was the only one to see the clown kill Nolan and break out. Walter is a mess, and the clown has escaped into the woods. We have an emergency situation on our hands. Walter requested to speak with you about the murder."

Dr. Roberts frantically said, "Search cell number four-ninety-nine on the fifth floor! Officer Burnes was in charge of escorting McRandle to his cell! We need to investigate this mess! I want to speak with Walter before the manhunt for McRandle begins!"

Officer Jones hustled up to the fifth floor as Dr. Roberts headed to the cell containing the paranoid McFrancis. Dr. Roberts knocked on the door of McFrancis's cell and said, "Walter, it's me, Dr. Roberts. You said you wanted to speak with me." Dr. Roberts entered the cell to have a private conversation with McFrancis. The doctor noticed that Walter was very nervous and breathing awkwardly. The doctor decided to play a mind game with the nervous patient and pretended to be his friend. The doctor calmly said, "Walter, come take a walk down around the corner to my office. Let me get you a glass of water. You seem thirsty and this might help calm you down."

Walter said, "Thank you, Dr. Roberts. I need a glass of water. My throat is very dry."

Dr. Roberts said, "It's OK, Walter. You're not in any trouble. Come along now." The two of them took a walk around the corner and into the office. Walter was still breathing awkwardly. However, he seemed a little calmer than he had been a few minutes ago. Dr. Roberts coddled Walter some more as he told him to take a seat and control his breathing. Roberts poured the patient a glass of water and told him to take a drink. The nervous patient took a few swigs of water and coughed. Dr. Roberts said, "So, Walter, can you tell me what you saw? Don't be nervous. I'm your friend, and I'm here to help you."

Walter said, "I saw the clown stab Officer Nolan with something. I can't get the horror out of my mind. It was terrible. I saw the clown escape and vanish into the forest from my bedroom window."

Roberts replied, "That's terrible, Walter. Officer Nolan was a good man, and his son was born just last week. I'll have Officer Jones inform his wife. I hate giving good people bad news. As for us, I need you to take a journey with me into the forest. You're the only one who saw the clown."

Walter nervously replied, "Dr. Roberts, I can't face the demons of the dark forest. It gives me the creeps. I'm not as brave as you are. I don't have the courage. Please don't make me go out there."

The warden could hear the footsteps of Officer Jones hustling down the hallway and said, "I'll be right back, Walter. Sit tight for just a minute. I have to speak with Officer Jones now, all right?" Walter wiped the tears off his face and slowly nodded his head.

Officer Jones had recently confirmed the death of Officer Burnes. Once he reached the fifth floor, he rounded the corner and peeked inside of cell number four-ninety-nine. He saw Officer Burnes dead on the floor covered in a puddle of blood. The warden stepped out to the hallway for an update on the search. Officer Jones said to Dr. Roberts, "Sir, Officer Burnes has been killed in the line of duty. There were no witnesses present, but evidence indicates that McRandle could potentially be the one responsible for his murder."

The doctor said to Officer Jones, "I should have taken McRandle's threats more seriously. I underestimated just how resourceful one lunatic can be in a confined prison. McRandle had a vendetta against Burnes and Nolan after his arrest. There's no doubt in my mind that he's responsible for their murders. OK, here's the plan, Jones: I want all officers to remain stationary on their normal routine. However, you'll be promoted to warden and placed in my office while I'm gone. I'm going to take Walter into the forest with me on the McRandle manhunt."

Officer Jones said to the warden, "That's against our facility regulations. All prisoners must remain inside at all times."

Dr. Roberts angrily replied, "Fuck regulations! I'm in charge, and I'm calling the shots! We're throwing the shackles on the unstable bastard, and I'm taking him out there. I'll have my gun with me if things get dangerous with McRandle. Walter won't be a problem. He's too afraid of his own shadow. We have to make a man out of him sometime, and what better night than Halloween? I'm going in the other room, and I'm going to shackle this pussy up and take him out into the forest. I need his help with the search. He was a key eyewitness. Keep your suggestions concerning the building regulations to yourself or else I'll withdraw your temporary promotion!"

Officer Jones slowly put his head down in shame. The persistent warden walked back into his office and grabbed a pair of shackles from out of his drawer. The doctor said, "OK, Walter, I'm going to shackle you up, and we're going to take a journey into the forest to find Herman, the clown."

Walter said, "No, please, I don't want to go out there," as he nervously shook in the corner.

Dr. Roberts said, "It's OK, friend. I have my gun, and I'll protect us both. Please help me find the clown."

Walter replied, "I'll go with you to help you find the clown as long as you keep me safe, friend."

The doctor slowly shackled Walter. The doctor awkwardly hesitated for a few seconds then looked sincerely into the eyes of McFrancis and said to him, "I promise to keep you safe, friend." After Walter was shackled up, the doctor said to him, "Look, Walter, I have a lantern with me. I know that the dark forest makes you nervous, so this will help us see."

Walter twitched a little and replied, "I'm ready to face the forest now. Let's go find the clown."

Dr. Roberts said, "That's the good old Irish spirit, Walter. Let's take a journey into the forest and find the clown." The warden and Walter exited the private office. Officer Jones was still waiting outside of the warden's office. The warden said to Officer Jones, "You're in charge now, Officer Jones."

Officer Jones said, "Sir, I apologize for my comments concerning the building regulations. I'll keep things under control around here while you're on the McRandle manhunt."

Dr. Roberts said, "Your apology is accepted, Officer Jones. We've all made mistakes tonight. I'm guilty of diverting some of our manpower to the Dublin Halloween Fair. As a result, we're slightly understaffed here. We mustn't panic, though. When I report back, I'll have you notify Burnes's and Nolan's next of kin. We'll take time to grieve for their deaths after the McRandle manhunt is over. I'll capture that green-haired psychopath, come hell or high water!"

Walter was standing and shaking uncontrollably in the hallway. He was nervous about the task that lay ahead of him. He agreed to help the warden with the search, although the thought of the clown in the forest was one of his worse fears imaginable. The warden and McFrancis both left the asylum and walked in the direction of the forest where the clown was last seen.

CHAPTER 8

McRandle was already far ahead of Dr. Roberts and McFrancis. When McRandle was a few hundred yards behind the graveyard, he recklessly fired his stolen ammunition into the trees when he was spooked by a ghost. When McRandle fired six shots into the trees, the ghost faded away into thin air. His stolen handgun no longer contained ammunition and was rendered useless, so he ditched it in the woods. The confused McRandle stood in the woods and gazed at the dark trees as he wondered what the hell it was he just saw. What the drunken McRandle saw in the trees was a brief glimpse of the Ghost of Cornelius haunting the Dublin woods.

Dr. Roberts knew that a little time was wasted in order to calm Walter down and get him to assist with the McRandle manhunt. During the first five minutes of the search, Dr. Roberts was using his lantern and trying to follow McRandle's clown footprints. The exact whereabouts of the clown was a mystery that had Dr. Roberts puzzled. McFrancis was shaking like a little girl the further they walked into the Dublin woods.

McRandle was further down the mountainside and further from the asylum. Along his travels he giggled and thought that his escape route was flawless. When he took a few more steps down the mountainside, he walked directly under a giant tree. Once under the tree, a mysterious man saw him from under the branches. This man pulled a knife from his pocket as he approached McRandle. He jumped down on McRandle, blindsiding him and took him to the ground. The mysterious man grunted heavily as he quickly and forcefully decapitated the clown with his knife. Herman's escape route was no longer perfect. This mysterious man grabbed the head of the clown and put it in his small duffel bag and vanished from the area unseen. The man left behind the dead body of McRandle while bringing his duffel bag containing his newest trophy. He walked further down the mountainside and headed to the high peak riverbed located a mile away.

Five minutes passed as Dr. Roberts and the nervous Walter were heading near the giant tree where the clown had been recently murdered. Walter looked to his left and saw McRandle's body under a giant tree. Walter frantically pointed over to the body and yelled, "Dr Roberts, I found the clown, and he lost his head!"

The doctor pointed his gun around the crime scene. He walked over and pointed the lantern in the direction of the clown. As Roberts walked a little closer, the frantic Walter started to keel over and cry. Roberts saw the dead clown and that the head was missing. He wondered to himself for a minute what had just happened and whether someone was indeed stalking him. He took a look around and saw no strangers in plain sight. The doctor searched around the dead body for more evidence. The evidence next to the bloody body was some broken branches, fragments of torn clown clothing, and a set of footprints. The mysterious man who killed McRandle left a trail of footprints from his boots.

Thomas Roberts knew that he had a chance to investigate this problem and get to the bottom of it. Roberts held his gun in his right hand and his lantern in his left hand as he walked over to calm Walter again. Dr. Roberts said, "It's OK, friend. I will protect us." Walter hugged the doctor. The doctor said to McFrancis, "Now, now, Walter. Let's be men. We need to walk quietly a little further and see if anyone else is in the forest. Stay close by and tell me if you see someone."

Dr. Roberts led the way as Walter followed. The doctor tried his best to follow the path of the new set of footprints. The two men now walked the Dublin trail in search of a mysterious murderer.

CHAPTER 9

Meanwhile, it had been about an hour since Mick Patrican had murdered O'Neill and O'Connor. The massive manhunt was still on as thirty forest-dwelling murderers searched all along the Dublin trails. Patrican had been hiding at the bottom of a hill, and he hadn't moved in a while. He was cautious to move because one of the guards had been pacing back and forth for quite some time. The Dublin guard flashed his lantern and peeked up the hill. Patrican slowly and quietly crawled behind a rock to avoid being spotted. The guard looked over in that section and saw nothing but a rock. The guard decided to walk further down the trail instead of searching the hill. As Mr. Patrican lay behind the rock unspotted, the guard vanished from his sight. Mick decided to take cover for a few more minutes as the lunatic walked further down the trail.

The next thing Mick noticed was a bright, green light that came from out of nowhere and glowed right next to him. This glowing green light suddenly appeared to Patrican in the form of a ghost. Mick nervously drew out his small fishing knife and prepared to protect himself. The supernatural ghost told Patrican not to fear him and that he was a guide for him. Patrican took a few deep breaths and put the knife back in the pocket of his army pants. Mick said to the ghost, "Who are you? I heard your voice earlier tonight. You were the one who was warning me and my brothers to turn back."

The ghost floated and replied, "That's right, Mr.Patrican. I was the voice of friendly warning that you and your brothers should have listened to. I'm sorry that your brothers did not survive the attack. I was General Butch McPherson.

53

I'm showing myself for the first time ever to you and to you alone. The reason for this is you are a unique person.

"You and I have something in common. We're the only two people who have defeated the mummy in his two thousand years of existence. You've survived longer than anyone could've ever imagined possible in the evil forest. Thirty lunatics are on a massive manhunt for you. So far, they've failed to capture you. I have seen the history of these trails for over the last two thousand years. I was the Irish soldier who killed the mummy in the Irish-Egyptian war.

"The Egyptians ambushed our land in an attempt to dominate Ireland. Irish troops outnumbered and outlasted the Egyptians and won the war. There were many casualties on both sides of the battle. I was the last surviving soldier to live on this turf. This is why my spirit is able to live on. The lunatic's fortressing these grounds are unaware of my existence. They are permanently blind from this voice or vision, as they see and hear only evil. My ability to see into the future is not nearly as clear as my ability to see into the past. You will run into a new threat of danger upon your exit attempt from the trail. This man is more dangerous than you could ever imagine. He is a murderous Irish fisherman who will try to take you out. The fisherman is an expert at blindside kills, so you must be careful. I can't tell you if you will survive or not, so your fate is completely up to you. Now that I have revealed my true self to you, you will never be able to see or hear me again. I must go now and vanish forever. Good luck, Mr. Patrican." The bright, green ghost vanished into thin air as Patrican kept his eyes wide open in utter shock.

Patrican softly uttered the words, "Thank you, General McPherson," as he felt comforted and overwhelmed at the same time. Patrican continued to lay low for a moment. He knew that he had to flee the Dublin woods, but he did not know the safest way out. Mick decided to make his way up the hill slowly and quietly. As a few minutes passed, he was about halfway up the top. He decided to take a breather and regain some energy.

CHAPTER 10

At the high peak of the trail, there was a small riverbed that the fisherman entered by way of a tiny fishing boat. The fisherman had docked his boat there a short time before his killing of the clown. Not much was known about this shady and mysterious man. One could say that, literally, in the sense that his real name was unknown to all. He was abandoned by his birth mother in a cradle at sea on October 13, 1850. He was eventually rescued by a group of murderous Irish fishermen. They taught this child to be evil to the innocent. They trained him to be a stone-cold killer on land and at sea. The vicious Irish fishermen also trained this man to kill and to vanish from the crime scene.

The fisherman had murdered a few people on the Irish seas. The authorities had no leads or witnesses of the mysterious murders at sea. The fisherman sought this new land to murder by the Dublin River. He wanted to test his limits with new fishing and hunting opportunities. The fisherman never served any time in prison or in the insane asylum. The fisherman was a rugged man, weighing about 225 pounds. The fisherman knew that the Dublin woods were a dangerous place. The fisherman arrogantly felt as though he was the most dangerous new threat the trail had ever faced.

The Irish fisherman lit up a victory cigar as he took in the tobacco, tasting success from the McRandle kill. He said, "Ah, that's the sweet taste of a victory kill! The clown put up no fight against me! Fuck the clown! He was a wimp, and I decapitated him! That's right. I'm the evil fisherman, and I decapitate my victims with my fishing knife! I rule the Dublin River and anywhere that I embark upon! I have a collection of decapitated heads!"

As he grabbed McRandle's head from out of his duffel bag, he laughed with an evil sound and said, "The clown head! My newest trophy!" The fisherman pointed at his duffel bag and said, "I've got two more heads in my duffel bag. I cut off their heads on the Irish seas last month. I've got a few more heads in my boat, but I'm prouder of these three latest kills. I fear no one who roams the Dublin trails! How about a second or a third kill for me on this epic Halloween night! Come on, who's next?"

The fisherman put McRandle's decapitated skull back into his duffel bag. He took a chug of his whiskey bottle and a drag of his cigar. He finished off his whiskey and stomped out his cigar and started to gather sticks and rocks to build a small fire pit. Once the fire pit was together, he struck a match and lit the fire. As the fire slowly started to burn and smoke up, the fisherman heard a small noise a short distance away. The man drew out his fishing knife and slowly crept with cautious eyes to the area where he heard the noise. The bushes started to shake as the fisherman crept toward them. Mick Patrican had now reached the top of the hill. Once Patrican stood up, he and the fisherman looked each other square in the eyes. The distance between the two of them was five feet. The fisherman pointed his knife at Patrican and said, "You're dead!"

Patrican drew out his slightly smaller fishing knife and said, "Fuck you, asshole!" They both charged toward each other, and the battle was on.

The fisherman swung his knife right toward Patrican's throat. Mick managed to slide back and duck his body under the fisherman's attack. Patrican swung his knife and cut the fisherman's right hand and wrist. The fisherman immediately dropped his knife in the bushes. This was a brutal wound; however, the fisherman groaned in pain and kept fighting. He punched Patrican in the face with his left hand. Patrican dropped his knife as he fell on the ground and into the bushes. The fisherman jumped into the bush to attack Patrican. The two enemies rolled around and wrestled in the bush looking for the knives.

The fisherman started to strangle Mick with his bloody hand. Patrican started to gasp for air as the fisherman was searching the bushes with his left hand for one of the lost knives. Patrican noticed that the fisherman managed to grab hold of a knife. Just before the fisherman could slice Patrican's throat, Mick drew his left elbow back and into the fisherman's sternum. The fisherman got the wind knocked out of him for a second and dropped the knife into the bushes. Patrican turned around and punched the fisherman in the face with a quick right hook.

The fisherman dropped into the bushes as Patrican fell on him. They struggled to force each other off of the hill near the bush. As they were both trying to throw each other off the hill, they both tried to stay on level ground.

The fisherman out-muscled Mick and was in a position to throw him off the hill. Patrican's feet dangled down the hill as he held tightly onto the fisherman's neck. The fisherman was trying to reach in the bush for one of the lost knives. Seconds later, he grabbed ahold of a knife inside the bushes. The fisherman swung the blade close to Patrican's throat. This attempt failed when Patrican managed to block the hand with the swinging blade, causing the fisherman to drop his knife down the hill. Patrican punched the fisherman in the face with a quick jab from his right fist. Mick was still gripping the fisherman's neck with his left hand. The fisherman shook himself free and drew back into the bushes. As Patrican got up, he put up his two fists and approached the fisherman. The fisherman quickly moved both of his arms around in the bushes in hopes of finding the other knife. The fisherman managed to find Patrican's knife and held it up. The fisherman moved around with the knife while Patrican held up his two fists. These two rugged men were now fighting more toward middle ground. About five feet to their left was a ten-foot drop into a shallow part of the river.

The doctor and Walter were traveling a few minutes away and could see a small fire and smoke rising in the dark air. They both walked a little further, and the doctor said he could hear heavy breathing. The doctor said, "Let's quietly move over this way, Walter. I can see a fire, and I hear voices over in this direction."

Walter drooled and nervously twitched a few times and said, "OK, Dr. Roberts." They walked quickly in the direction of the fire. Patrican was still ducking and dodging the fisherman's knife swipes. From the corner of Mick's eye, he saw the clown's head roll out of the duffel bag. The clown's head lay sideways on the ground as his jaw started to move and speak. The evil voodoo spirit of Herman McRandle said to Patrican, "Hey, Patrican, I want revenge on the fisherman! Only you can hear me! The fisherman killed me! I'm dead to him! You cut off his fuckin' head! If you fail me, I'll make sure your body rots out here forever just like your brothers'!"

Patrican tried his best to focus on the fight instead of the terrible voice of the haunting clown. McRandle's voodoo curse from the afterlife gave him visions of the haunted trail's violent past. His hazel-colored demon eyes could see the brutal executions of Patrican's older brothers. The doctor appeared from out of nowhere and shot the fisherman in the abdomen. The fisherman groaned in pain as he dropped off the ten-foot ledge and into the shallow riverbed. Patrican noticed that the doctor was aiming the gun at him now, so he decided to bail down the hill. The doctor shot at Patrican, and he managed to hit the back of his right thigh with a silver bullet. When the doctor and Walter moved toward him, Patrican rolled far down the hill and vanished from range. Patrican rolled down the hill a few hundred feet as trees and rocks stopped his momentum. The fisherman groaned in pain from down in the shallow riverbed and shouted, "I'm shot! I need a doctor!"

As Dr. Roberts and Walter stared down at the injured fisherman, the clown's head started to speak to them. The cursed clown said, "Hey, Roberts, it's me, Herman McRandle, the evil clown!"

The doctor said, "So the evil curse that you claimed from the afterlife is true after all. The rumors of some of our former patients residing out here in the Dublin woods also appear to be true."

The clown said, "I got my revenge on Burnes and Nolan, but the fisherman killed me! I want the fisherman's fuckin' head! I'll fuck with you for life unless you give me what I want! Roberts, I want you and that fuckin' pussy to grab the fishing net from the fisherman's boat. Then you use that fuckin' net to drag the fisherman up to level ground! Then you drag him a mile due west until you reach the guillotine! Don't you fail me, Dr. Roberts! I want my fuckin' revenge!"

Dr. Roberts knew that he had no choice other than to comply with the cursed clown's evil demands. The doctor told the jittery Walter to take a stroll with him over to the fisherman's boat and grab the fishing net. The boat was docked on a muddy area of a shallow part of the Dublin riverbed. It took Walter and Dr. Roberts a minute to get to the boat as Roberts shined the lantern ahead. When Roberts put the lantern down for a second, he realized that his backup set of six silver bullets had gone missing from his possession. The doctor looked in the six-round chamber of his gun and saw that he had only one bullet left. Thomas Roberts knew that he had to be conservative and accurate with his one bullet. Dr. Roberts said to Walter, "Damn it, Walter, stop twitching. You're acting like a little girl. I need you to be a man and help me with the fishing net. Your incompetence is really starting to piss me off."

McFrancis replied, "I'm sorry, Dr. Roberts. I'm so nervous out here in the forest. I'll try to be brave."

Dr. Roberts and the crying Walter grabbed the net and climbed down the hill to the wounded fisherman. With a burning silver bullet bleeding around his abdomen, the fisherman knew that he was now defenseless. The doctor looked down at the wounded fisherman and kicked him in the face three times. Between the forceful kicks to the skull and the bullet wound, the fisherman was knocked unconscious. The doctor commanded the nervous Walter to help him wrap up the unconscious fisherman in the fishing net. They pulled his body up and rolled it into the fishing net. After that they both dragged his body up jagged rocks and rough terrain. Within a short time, they had reached level ground. Dr. Roberts said, "Thank you for your assistance, Walter. You are no longer necessary."

The doctor cracked the butt of his gun directly on the skull of the shackled mental patient. Walter was dazed and lost his balance, falling down the hillside opposite of the riverbed. McFrancis started to cry and panic as he rolled down the hill in shackles. After rolling down the hill a few hundred feet, his body took a devastating blow from a thick-barked tree. The tree stopped his momentum, breaking his ribs in addition to his serious head wound. McFrancis had cuts and bruises all over his body and was in need of serious medical attention. Walter frantically yelled, "No! Doctor Roberts, you said that you were my friend and that you were going to protect me! Doctor Roberts, I need help! Save me, Lerman!" Walter was severely injured, and he had a speech impediment, so he desperately said, "Save me, Lerman," referring to Herman, the haunting clown.

The doctor betrayed Walter because he was annoyed by his whining and sniveling manner. The doctor said, "Why waste my last silver bullet on a fuckin' pussy?" The doctor grabbed the decapitated skull of Herman McRandle and placed it in the fishing net. He looked at his compass and walked due west, dragging the heavy fishing net along with him as he headed down the slope of the mountainside.

Herman was determined to witness the successful decapitation of the fisherman. Herman said to the doctor, "Hurry up and get a move on! This area will be swarming with guards soon with that whimpering pussy you just gun bucked!" The doctor ran as he dragged the injured fisherman and Herman's decapitated skull away from the noisy area. They headed due west by the doctor's compass and in the direction of the guillotine.

Walter, still crying loudly, had fully drawn attention to his exact whereabouts. Two mentally ill guards spotted him and ran over in his direction. Walter cried and said, "I need help. Are you here to save me?"

One of the mental guards replied, "No! We're here to kill you!"

Walter kept crying, "No!" The two mental guards dragged him by his shackled feet to the bottom of the hill. His screams suddenly stopped for a second as he attempted to shake his way free but was unsuccessful. The shackles and his previous injuries prevented his escape. He was dragged for a few minutes down a secluded path until it ended. All that surrounded this path was a patch of grass and more trees. There was a fire pit burning and Walter could see the foundation of a shack and a hanging pendulum.

CHAPTER 11

The designer of the pendulum and resident of the small shack was Martin Killington. Martin was responsible for the horrific Halloween massacre of 1842. Martin resided on a more secluded section of the Dublin trails than his twin brother Matthew. The Killington brothers were infamous. Martin and his brother Matthew were identical twins who shared the same look of evil. Matthew Killington was born six minutes before Martin Killington. The day these two evil bastards were born was October 31, 1827. One could literally call both of them bastards as their father abandoned them at birth. Their mother committed suicide by hanging herself when her husband left her and their newborn twins behind.

The Killington brothers were abandoned downtown just around the corner from Flanagan's Irish pub. Concerned locals walking the streets of Dublin soon noticed this and came to their aid. The Killington brothers were taken care of and brought to an orphanage in downtown Dublin. They developed violent tendencies at a young age due to the neglect by their parents. They lashed out at the six other orphans and bullied them around. The orphans feared the Killington brothers more than ever. The Killington brothers carried their dark past from birth into their adulthood. Today they turned sixty-five. They were both gray-haired with old bones, and they both had a decrepit hunchback. Martin had not had a trespasser roam in his neck of the woods in a little over two years.

Walter was dragged to the pendulum against his will and strapped down by the two guards as tears poured from his eyes and pain rushed throughout his body. Martin's face lit up with a sick smile as an unknown intruder had just trespassed on his patch of ground. Walter knew now that he was going to die.

Martin said, "At ease, gentlemen. Let us take a moment of silence before this Halloween execution." The moment of silence was interrupted by Walter's whimpers. The two guards and Martin were angered over this. Walter kept on whimpering as he was placed beneath the pendulum blade. He couldn't stop whimpering. Martin yelled in Walter's face and said, "How dare you make noise during my requested moment of silence! I'll make you shut the fuck up, you whimpering pussy!"

Martin grabbed a metal rod and walked toward the small fire near his shack. Martin placed the metal rod inside of the blazing fire. After about a minute, the rod became as hot as the fire itself. Martin walked back to the pendulum. Martin Killington placed the scalding hot metal rod directly over Walter's mouth. After Killington pressed the scalding metal rod on his face for nearly ten seconds, Walter's lip and tongue had been completely melted. Walter was now desperately fighting for air through his nose. Martin took the burning metal rod off of Walter's face as melting flesh started to peel from his mouth. Martin tossed the metal rod to the ground and said, "At ease, gentlemen. Let us take a second attempt at this moment of silence before this Halloween execution."

The night was practically silent with the exception of the small amount of breathing coming from Walter's nose. None of the three guards could hear Walter making any more noise so they prepared to take a second moment of silence. The three guards remained silent as a brief moment of time passed. Martin shouted to Walter, "Any last words before your execution!" It was obvious that the victimized Walter was unable to speak. The three men laughed after Killington made a sick execution joke. As the guards got serious again, Martin grabbed a rope and lowered the pendulum down a foot. He grabbed a separate rope connected to the pendulum blade. Martin began to move the rope and sway the pendulum blade slowly across Walter's throat. As Killington swung the pendulum blade back and forth, it started to drop slightly in elevation. The pendulum hadn't cut him yet, but would once it dropped another inch. Walter now took the last bits of air in from his nose along with the last sights and sounds he would ever experience on this very earth. The pendulum was now lowered one more inch, and it swiped across poor Walter's throat, finally killing him. Blood instantly splattered all over the pendulum blade.

Martin Killington's night was now complete. It had been a few years since his last execution, and he celebrated with evil pride knowing that tonight was the fiftieth anniversary of the Halloween massacre of 1842. The three evil men stood there as Killington said, "Ha, what a fuckin' pussy!" The three mental guards laughed with an evil sound as Martin Killington made another sick execution joke.

CHAPTER 12

Meanwhile the doctor dragged the fisherman. The doctor had been walking the unguarded due west path, and was approaching the guillotine that lay just ahead. The clown said, "You got to take out the Killington brother with your last silver bullet! Then you need to operate his guillotine to decapitate the fisherman and give me my trophy!"

The doctor replied, "I understand the purpose of my mission, Mr. McRandle. It would be an honor to assassinate one of the infamous Killington brothers."

The fisherman slowly regained consciousness and was very dazed and confused. He had a concussion from all of the blows that he received to his skull. The silver bullet that was once burning in his abdomen had cooled down a little. He was still in pain as blood gushed from his abdomen. The bullet was still lodged in his body, wreaking havoc with his internal organs. The fisherman yelled, "No! I'm losing blood! I need a doctor!"

Dr. Roberts pointed his gun at the fisherman and placed his finger along the trigger. He acted as if he was going to shoot the fisherman again. The doctor looked at the fisherman and said, "You have a doctor right here. Now quiet, you piece of shit. Your time is almost up."

The threat of another bullet caused the fisherman to stop talking without fuss. The fisherman started to lose the ability to realize what was going on. The guillotine station was a few hundred feet away, and the doctor's arms were becoming tired from the dragging. The clown started to speak again: "OK, Roberts, ditch the net here, and go in for the kill. Once Killington is dead you come back for me, and we'll finish this thing off."

Dr. Roberts complied with the clown's insane demands. There had been no sightings of Mick Patrican. Roberts assumed Mick was dead. As Dr. Roberts approached Matthew Killington, Matthew could not see the doctor. The doctor crept further along and noticed that Killington stood clueless by his station. Killington stood there with his arms crossed and had no idea he was about to be shot. The doctor got on his hands and knees and crawled a little closer to the guillotine. Roberts was still about one-hundred feet away. Dr. Roberts stood up as he pointed his gun at Killington and prepared to take his shot, trusting his shot from a distance. Matthew looked over from a distance and said, "Dr. Roberts."

Matthew noticed a man from a distance and had a feeling that it was he. The two had seen each other's faces many times before in the Dublin Mental Institution. Dr. Roberts kept Matthew Killington in line while he was a patient there. Before another word was spoken, Dr. Roberts pulled the trigger of his small handgun, and his last silver bullet was shot directly into Killington's forehead. The doctor assassinated one of the infamous Killington brothers. Matthew Killington was now dead. Now there was no one in sight of the guillotine station.

The doctor knew that the shot being fired might have drawn some attention, so he hurried back to the fishing net. Dr. Roberts knew that some of the guards had diverted their attention a mile away where Walter was screaming and crying. The doctor grabbed the fishing net and dragged it toward the guillotine. The clown smiled from inside the fishing net as he could see the guillotine only feet away. The fisherman regained consciousness yet again and saw the rustic setup of the guillotine and realized this was the last time he would ever have a head. The clown rolled his head from out of the fishing net and realized he would soon have a revenge trophy of his own.

Dr. Roberts forced the fisherman onto his hands and knees and strapped him into the guillotine. The fisherman shouted his last words: "No! Don't drop the blade on my neck! I'm already injured! I need a fuckin' doctor! No!"

Dr. Roberts dropped the blade of the guillotine, and the fisherman's head was decapitated, falling into a wooden bucket next to the guillotine. The clown started to praise the doctor. The clown said, "Nice kill, Roberts! That was fuckin' fantastic! Revenge is mine, fisherman! Now I've got your head as my trophy!"

No more than a second later, Patrican sneaked up from behind the shed and snapped Dr. Roberts's neck, and Roberts immediately fell to his death.

The clown spoke to Patrican and said, "Patrican, where the fuck did you come from? I thought you were dead!"

Patrican said, "Just tell me the safest way out of these fuckin' woods."

The clown said, "Go back up the steep hill, and head to the riverbed. You can take the fisherman's boat to a safe passage. You need to hurry up and stay unseen. There's an angry mob trying to hunt you down, and they're onto your whereabouts. I knew there was something unique about your survival skills. Thanks, Patrican, and good luck with your escape."

Patrican headed back up the steep hill and toward the fisherman's boat. His face was still streaked with mud. His mud-covered face and army clothing had temporarily kept him camouflaged and unspotted by the guards searching for him. He could hear the mob running from a great distance away but was now spotted, so he hustled up the hill, moving his legs as fast as humanly possible. After a few minutes of hard running, he reached the top of the hill. Patrican ran down to the riverbed and dragged the fisherman's boat into the river. Patrican began to paddle fast as arrows shot from a distance narrowly missed his skull. A few guards jumped into the river to swim after him. The Dublin Woods Protector was running from a great distance and trying to catch up. The evil guards had failed. Patrican managed to row the boat way out of sight from the lunatics in pursuit of him. As Mick paddled, the river started to get rough and choppy. There was not enough moonlight for Patrican to see ahead properly. Patrican became nervous. He knew he was in danger.

Back at the guillotine, the clown had a sick smile on his face. Herman McRandle's last words before his voodoo curse wore off and his evil spirit permanently died were, "Sorry, Patrican, I forgot to warn you about the waterfall! Happy Halloween! Ha! Ha! Ha! Ha! Ha!" The clown's evil spirit permanently died.

As the river got rougher, Patrican's boat started to tip forward. Patrican hit a fifty-foot waterfall, and the boat capsized and was shipwrecked. Patrican fell down the waterfall and broke both of his legs on jagged rocks. Mick hit the waterfall and submerged from the momentum of the powerful water. As he thrashed around, he fought to get air. Patrican managed to swim out of the water, even though he was severely injured, and struggled to crawl out of the river with his bloody hands and legs. Mick Patrican started to vomit blood and water as he lay there injured and stranded on the haunted trail of Dublin, Ireland, barely alive.

40766059R00042

Made in the USA
Charleston, SC
16 April 2015